JUNGLE DEATH-VOLLEY

For a full two minutes not a sound disturbed the jungle's stillness as the Black Eagles, their faces streaked with sweat and their lips tightly pursed together in dreaded anticipation, tried to catch sight of something—anything—through the brush that stretched down from their perimeter.

The attack burst forth when figures of Pathet Lao, who had painstakingly crawled dozens of meters through the rain forest, suddenly leaped up and charged, their high-pitched screaming eerie in the tight confinement of the jungle vegetation.

Falcon's men, with the former grenadiers now acting as automatic riflemen in their fire teams, cut loose with sweeping volleys that sent swarms of bullets slashing into the yelling Pathet Lao.

These fanatical storm troops threw up their arms, spinning and staggering under the impact of oncoming slugs. But behind them, their wild comrades contiued to push forward. . . .

#3
NIGHTMARE IN LAOS

THE BLACK EAGLES

BY JOHN LANSING

ZEBRA BOOKS
KENSINGTON PUBLISHING CORP.

ZEBRA BOOKS

are published by

Kensington Publishing Corp.
475 Park Avenue South
New York, NY 10016

First printing: March, 1984

Printed in the United States of America

This book is dedicated to *Major Roy H. Akridge, Jr.*

Special acknowledgment to Patrick E. Andrews

CHAPTER ONE

Specialist Fourth Class Orville Hanover, United States Army, had it made. It was 1964 and the conflict in far-away Vietnam seemed to be growing daily, but Orville had only eight months left to do until his two-year term of service as a draftee would be completed. Much too short a time to have to sweat being shipped overseas to the fighting.

And his job at Fort Dix, New Jersey was something to be envied too. As the TI&E NCO (Troop Information and Education Noncommissioned Officer) of a basic training battalion, he had little to do beyond seeing that his displays, set up in each of his unit's four companies, were kept up to date. These were no more than book and magazine racks with bulletin boards mounted above them. Orville made sure the latest newspapers and magazines were kept there for the troops' enjoyment, and he clipped special articles from them and posted those on the cork boards to draw attention to whatever information seemed important enough to affect the soldiers' morale and attitudes.

Orville's tasks took no more than three hours of his work day. When all these chores were finished, he would withdraw to his office located in one corner of the battalion supply annex building and pass the time smoking, dozing, and drinking Cokes while waiting for duty hours to end. Then he would make a beeline to head-quarters company's orderly room to pick up his pass and go to town. Orville had a hot little number working in a cafe just off post, and he liked to spend his free hours drinking coffee in the happy anticipation of all the good times waiting for him when she came off shift.

The only other addition to Orville's less than arduous duties was having to give a TI&E talk once a week to the battalion of recruits who were going through basic training. But the text of these talks was furnished by the army, so he did little more than read aloud to the dozing rookies, who were glad for the chance to get off their aching feet, before once more withdrawing to the sanctity of his little office.

But one day Specialist Fourth Class Orville Hanover's routine was interrupted.

He had returned to his office after bringing his TI&E boards up to date and found a note waiting for him. It instructed the young soldier to report immediately to the battalion sergeant major. Mildly curious, Orville left the supply annex and strolled nonchalantly down the street and presented himself to the unit's top kick.

The sergeant major, busy devouring a PX cheese-burger brought to him by a headquarters orderly, swallowed a mouthful, belched, and glared at the young man standing in front of him.

Orville was not the picture of military professionalism. Short, skinny, and stoop-shouldered, his thin face always seemed to bear a sort of quizzical expression. His fatigue uniform, no matter how starched and pressed, displayed a mind of its own, hanging on to its owner's body in a sloppy, sacklike manner.

The sergeant major grunted, "Report to S2 at

post headquarters."

"What does S2 want with me, Sergeant Major?" Orville asked wondering what the intelligence section of the staff would possibly desire to talk to him about.

"I don't know. They made a phone call, said to send you over there. Move your ass."

"Yes, Sergeant Major."

Orville took his time walking the few blocks up to the large building. He ran across a buddy who was processing out of the army and enviously listened to the guy's spiel on what he was going to do first when he got back home. Then Orville had a soft drink at the PX snack bar and ogled the girl with the big tits who served him. Talking to her only made him hornier for his girl friend at the cafe.

Finally, a good hour and a half after leaving the sergeant major, Orville meandered into headquarters and stopped at the staff duty NCO's desk. "My name's Spesh'list Orville Hanover. They say they want me at S2."

The noncom, a sleepy-eyed staff sergeant, pointed down the length of a long narrow hallway. "Last door on the left."

"Thanks, Sarge." Orville went to the place indicated and stopped at the door which bore a sign reading "S-2 Intelligence."

He rapped lightly and opened it in the prescribed manner. A bespectacled captain looked up at him. "Yes?"

"I'm Spesh'list Hanover, sir. My sergeant major said somebody here wanted to see me."

The captain displayed his best expression of annoyance. "Is that the way they taught you to report?"

Orville snapped to attention and saluted. "Spesh'list Hanover reporting as ordered, sir."

The captain returned the salute with his right hand while at the same time pointing over his shoulder with the left. "In there."

Again Orville knocked and stepped through a portal. Here he found, not an army man, but a civilian seated behind the desk with his feet propped up on it. He was reading *Playboy* and he glanced at Orville with a friendly expression. Then he flipped the magazine over and showed him the centerfold. "How do you like the boobs on that broad, huh?"

"Nice," Orville answered sincerely.

"Are you Hanover?" the man asked.

"Yeah," Orville answered. He'd be damned if he was going to report and salute some civilian.

The man smiled and offered his hand. "Howdy, my name is Fagin." He was a heavyset dark man in need of a closer shave. Balding and a bit unkempt, a cigarette dangled carelessly from the corner of his mouth. Fagin pulled a cardholder out of his suit jacket and flashed a government ID card. "Central Intelligence Agency." Fagin felt a bit odd showing the document since his branch of the government usually avoided them. But, in this case, it was thought to be necessary, so he displayed the blue-colored identification as he had been instructed to do.

"Yeah?"

"Yeah." He turned his attention from the girlie publication to the 201 personnel file sitting on the desk in front of him. He flipped the cardboard cover open and studied the documents in the interior for a few moments; then he closed it again. Fagin looked up at Orville. "We understand you're a licensed glider pilot."

"Sailplane pilot," Orville corrected him. "They're called sailplanes. We don't just gllide in 'em, you catch thermals—"

"Whatever," Fagin said uninterested. "You're supposed to be real good at . . . at flying *sailplanes*, right?"

"I won the Arizona State Junior Championship three years' running," Orville said. "Would've done it again, but I was in the fuckin' army."

"You been piloting them gliders, er, sailplanes for quite a while, huh?"

"Since I was sixteen," Orville said. "That's five years."

"Good. Just wanted to verify that. See that captain outside. Tell him you been verified."

"Verified?" Orville asked.

"Yeah—*verified*," Fagin said. Then he spoke slowly and distinctly. "Tell—the—officer—out—in—the—next—room—you've—been—verified."

"You mean the chickenshit guy with the glasses?"

"Right. G'bye, Hanover." The CIA man immediately returned his attention to the magazine.

"Sure. B'bye."

Orville went back to the outer office. He walked around to the front of the officer's desk and saluted again. "The guy in there said I was to tell you I've been . . . *ver—i—fied*."

"Be back here same time tomorrow with bag and baggage."

"Bag and baggage, sir?"

"Yeah. You're being transferred."

"Is the transfer off post, sir?"

The captain laughed. "It sure as hell is."

Orville saluted and stepped back through the door.

11

He paused in the hallway and thought over what had just happened. A feelilng of dread passed through his bony body.

"Shit!"

CHAPTER TWO

The Top was dead.

He had been blown away by the guns of a North Vietnamese infantry battalion during Operation Song Bo Slaughter over a month previously. Master Sergeant John Snow's death had dealt a crippling blow to the Black Eagles.

This special outfit operated directly under the command of SOG, Special Operations Group, out of South Vietnam. It had been organized for the express purpose of conducting highly dangerous, clandestine missions behind enemy lines. Made up of highly skilled and trained individualists of many nationalities and from every branch of the military units operating in Southeast Asia, the Black Eagles had completed two operations in their short history. Both had been successful, but casualties had been high.

The last job, which involved the rescue of POWs as well as the kidnapping of Communist interrogation experts, had proved the costliest. Particularly in light of the loss of Snow.

He had been the team sergeant, the senior noncommissioned officer who occupied a sensitive and responsible position in the chain of command. The men call him Top, a nickname that connoted respectful and admiring affection—and he had richly deserved such consideration.

Master Sergeant Snow, with his imposing, soldierly appearance, had been the picture of what a "team pappy" was supposed to look like. And his personality, which displayed great physical courage and other superb military qualities, completed the composite of what made a man's man.

Snow not only acted as the contact between officers and enlisted men, he also set the examples for them to follow, looked out for them like a worrisome old grandmother, and came down on their errant asses like ten tons of avenging angel when they fucked up.

Snow had done all those jobs admirably. A veteran combat fighter and excellent administrator, he held the detachment together with the force of his personality.

But Top was gone now, and the void he left was wide and empty.

The Black Eagles were stationed in a Special Forces "B" camp located in the boondocks north of Khe Sahn. Their commander, Captain Robert Falconi, had been dispatched to Saigon for a meet with their CIA case officer, and the remainder of the hardcore group waited for his return.

Sergeant Archie Dobbs, a veteran of seven years' service, was the detachment point man. Considered by many to be the best map-and-compass expert in the United States Army, Archie was a disciplinary problem. Without proper supervision he would drink heavily and smoke pot until his brain turned flip-flops in his skull. He was a short, blond man with heavy shoulders and arms. Although a bit bandy-legged he moved easily with near athletic prowess. Constantly being promoted and demoted, he also displayed a marked tendency to fight — particularly senior sergeants — but, even in his wildest fits, Archie had never considered striking Top. Not out of fear, but out of pure unadulterated respect.

The detachment demo was handled by newly promoted Staff Sergeant Calvin Culpepper. The tall, heavily muscled black man was a veteran soldier, twenty-seven years old with ten years of service in the army. A master at demolitions, he was as much at home with foreign mine warfare equipment as he was with American explosives. Although not a nervous man by nature, the type of work he did gave him a natural wariness of flamboyant or careless individuals. One of his favorite sayings was, "I don't care if I'm ever the *best* demo man in the U.S. Army, as long as I get to be the *oldest!*"

A Cherokee Indian, Sergeant First Class Jack Galchaser handled the unit's intelligence chores. Nicknamed Horny by the others, Galchaser was barrel-chested, six feet, two inches of Special Forces paratrooper. Despite his monicker, Horny was a devoted family man with a wife and three children waiting for him back in Fayetteville, North Carolina. One of his most outstanding talents was as an aerial photo interpreter.

The supply side of the operations was in the capable hands of a marine staff sergeant named Liam O'Quinn. Known as Lightfingers, O'Quinn was the best scrounger in Southeast Asia. If he couldn't draw, steal, trade for, or make a bribe to get a particular item of equipment, it was because the thing hadn't been invented yet. Short, husky, and fond of food, it was obvious he would grow quite heavy in his later years. But serving in the Black Eagles kept his girth under a semblance of control at least, while he worried and stewed to make sure each and every man was fully and properly equipped. Short-tempered, humorless, and curt, he was the hardest worker of the Black Eagles.

If any of the men had medical problems, they took them to Sergeant First Class Malcolm McCorckel. "Malpractice" McCorckel was as much a mother hen as Top had been. He saw to it that the men followed the most rigid sanitary and medical regulations as he stewed about everything from flea bites to bubonic plague. A fully qualified Special Forces medic, Malpractice could — and, indeed, did — perform war surgery under rugged emergency circumstances.

The final member of the team was the most unusual. Although Nguyen Van Dow held a first lieutenant's commission in the South Vietnamese Army, he had once been a dedicated and effective member of the Viet Cong, fighting fiercely against the very side and cause he now served. At present, he was the executive officer of the Black Eagles, having taken the position as second in command at the death of Lieutenant Ritchie Wakely in the last operation.

Dinky Dow was a little guy, only five feet, three inches tall and weighing in at a staggering one hundred and twenty pounds. He had lost his fervor for socialism when his fiancée had been brutally raped by a regional commissar and then forced to serve as a "joy girl," as official prostitutes were known. He now fought with a near insane fanaticism against his former comrades and with such intensity that the other Black Eagles referred to him as Dinky Dow — Vietnamese for crazy.

Dinky Dow and Top had enjoyed a special relationship. The young ex-VC had displayed not only the usual Oriental reverence and deference toward an older per-son, but he had learned to trust in the sergeant's wisdom and advice. Dinky Dow had taken Top's death very badly. His hatred for the antagonists up north had leaped tenfold, and he had sworn to kill a thousand to avenge Top.

These six men and their commander were all that made up the Black Eagles. The outfit now awaited new assignments and the attachment of other specialists in the grim warfare they conducted, while their commanding officer was in Saigon getting briefed on their next mission.

A half a world away from the troubles in Southeast Asia, a guard, assigned to the prison garage in the Texas State Penitentiary, walked over to answer the telephone ringing on his desk. He listened to the terse and quick words spoken to him; then he hung up and walked out into the shop where convict mechanics were servicing various state vehicles brought in for repair.

He approached one of the prisoners and tapped him on the shoulder. The man looked up from under the hood of the pickup truck he was working on.

"Yes, sir Mister Martin?"

"Yo're wanted up to the warden's office, Beamer."

"Yes, sir."

"Straighten up and wash the grease off them hands o' yores," the guard said. "I don't want the warden thinkin' I'm lettin' you sonofabitches git sloppy, heah?"

"Yes, sir, Mister Martin."

Beamer went over to a nearby sink and turned on the water. Using strong lye soap, the convict scrubbed the grease and oil off his hands and arms as best he could. After drying off he went outside and reported at the gate

17

leading to the prison's main building to begin the entrance procedure.

After enduring searches, metal detectors, and surly looks from the guards, Beamer was escorted up to the second-floor office of the warden. When he stepped into the carpeted room, Beamer saw that there was another man besides the penitentiary chief waiting for him.

The warden wasted no time. "Beamer, this here's Mister Fagin. He wants to talk to you." Then he abruptly left.

Beamer was a bit confused by the action. Usually the warden was completely and wholly in charge of things. His deference toward the stranger was most unusual and put the convict on his guard.

Fagin, who had been sitting in an easy chair on one side of the desk, got up and motioned Beamer to sit down. He walked around and took the warden's place. "How you doing, Mister Beamer?" He offered the prisoner a cigarette.

"About fifty years," Beamer answered sullenly, but he took the smoke. He was wiry young man, with close-cropped blond hair and blue eyes that were beginning to show a toughness after a year on prison.

"How old were you when they put you in the slammer?" Fagin asked in a direct manner.

"Twenty-seven," Beamer answered.

"Get out when you're seventy-seven, huh?"

"Looks like it."

"According to your record, you've only got the one conviction. No prior arrests, except a couple of traffic tickets," Fagin remarked.

"Yeah," Beamer said. "But possessing a coupla joints is real serious stuff here in Texas. I got twenty-five years for each of 'em — without possibility of parole."

"And your record also indicates that you've had military service," Fagin remarked. "And that included combat in Korea."

"Yeah," Beamer said. "I was a radio operator with the 2nd Division — 24th Infantry. I thought the army was bad 'til I ended up in prison."

"Boy! I'll bet you'd like to get the hell outta here, huh?"

Beamer ignored the question.

"You built gliders before you were sent here, right?"

"They were sailplanes," Beamer corrected him. "There's a difference —"

"Sure, I understand all that. You built your own, is that correct?"

Beamer was confused. "Yeah. I designed and flew some. Never made much money at it though. The low demand for sailplanes hardly warrants setting up mass production and assembly lines, does it?"

"I guess not," Fagin said. "I understand you made damned good ones though."

"A couple of mine won the Arizona State Championships. But I didn't pilot them. I got a hotshot young kid to fly in the competition."

"Flown by a young fellow named Orville Hanover, I believe."

"That's right."

Fagin picked up a briefcase he had stashed behind the warden's desk. He pulled out some bluprints and tossed them over to the convict. "What do you think of these?"

Beamer unfolded the sheets and studied them. "This ain't a sailplane, it *is* a glider."

"Right," Fagin said. "The Waco CG-4A to be exact. They used them about twenty years ago in World War

19

II. D-day. Holland and all those places the airborne troops fought."

"Mmmm," Beamer mused still studying the diagrams. "I'd say if you used fiberglass instead o' that fabric to cover the fuselage, then tapered and lengthened the wings, you could extend the glide ratio of this thing from about one-to-ten, to one-to-fifteen maybe."

"What's that mean, Beamer?"

"That would mean that if it could get one-to-fifteen, it would glide forward fifteen feet for every foot it sunk," the prisoner explained.

"Could you make one of those?" Fagin asked.

"At my workshop, yes," Beamer answered.

"What if a place was set up for you?"

"Where? Here?" Beamer asked.

Now it was Fagin's turn to ignore questions. "I want your assurance you can build one of these things."

"You seem to know my background," Beamer said. "That ought to be assurance enough." He stared suspiciously at the man across from him. "Who the hell are you, Mister?"

Fagin smiled slightly. "The son of a bitch who's going to get you out of jail."

CHAPTER THREE

The H-34 chopper eased down to the landing pad, sending stinging swirls of dust whipping into the half-dozen men standing there. They turned away as another six disembarked from the aircraft. After the passengers were all on the ground with their baggage, the helicopter's rotors increased in rpm and the pilot beat his way back into the sky to fly back to Saigon.

The new arrivals were a mixed group. The various uniforms they wore showed the men to be from a variety of military outfits. The one with the most outstanding features was a tall, dark man wearing the uniform of a Special Forces master sergeant. Humorless and severe he led the others over to the reception committee. "I'm looking for Lieutenant Nguyen," he announced.

Dinky Dow stepped forward and offered his hand. "I am Lieutenant Nguyen, second in command of Black Eagles."

The tall sergeant snapped to attention and saluted; then he bent slighty forward so that he could look down at the Vietnamese. "Master Sergeant Duncan Gordon, team sergeant, reporting for duty, sir."

Dinky Dow waved an informal salute and still insisted on shaking hands. "Glad to know you, Sergeant. Everybody call me Dinky Dow."

"I see." Gordon looked at the men behind Dinky Dow

without hiding his disapproval. The other Black Eagles—in various stages of dress and undress—were standing nonchalantly, waiting to see what would happen next. The sergeant turned his attention back to Dinky Dow. "I suggest we retire to the detachment bunker, sir. That way all team members can introduce themselves."

"Sure! Good idea, Sergeant," Dinky Dow said agreeably. He looked at the others and waved. "Hey, guys, you come! We go to bunker and say howdy! Drink beer and . . ." He stopped talking annd stared at one of the new arrivals. Then he grinned. "You the SAS guy, right?"

Staff Sergeant Tom Newcomb of the Australian SAS nodded and smiled. He walked over and offered his hand. "Good to see you again, Dinky Dow." He turned to the others. "And how are you, mates?"

Archie Dobbs offered his hand and slapped the Aussie on the shoulder. "Good to see you again, Tommy."

"It's *always* great to see you," Calvin Culpepper said, walking up with his large hand extended. "Especially after you pulled our asses outta all that shit awhile back."

"Just doing me job, mates," Newcomb said modestly as he exchanged greetings with Lightfingers, Malpractice, and Horny. "And I'm glad to be posted with you blokes."

"The feeling is definitely mutual," Malpractice McCorckel said.

"I see we're not all strangers," Gordon said coldly.

"Oh, no!" Dinky Dow exclaimed. "That Sergeant Newcomb. He help us out in Operation Song Bo Slaughter."

"Shall we go to the bunker, sir?" Gordon asked.

"Sure. Hey, call me Dinky Dow."

"No, thank you, sir."

The group, with the new men carrying their gear, walked down from the landing pad and hurried across the open area to a fortified section that boasted a sandbagged bunker. When everyone was inside, Dinky Dow held up his hand for attention. "Okay. I tell you new guys I am Dinky Dow, executive officer. Now I give you to the new team sergeant."

Duncan Gordon stepped forward. "I think the first order of business would be to organize the detachment as quickly as possible. I spoke with Captain Falconi yesterday and he must remain in Saigon until our new CIA case officer arrives to brief him on the next mission. In the meantime you'll get a chance to know me, and what I require from you in my job as the new team sergeant."

Archie Dobbs, scowling, lit a cigarette. "We're already organized. The Top done that months ago."

"What's your name?" Gordon demanded.

"Dobbs."

"You have a rank, Dobbs?"

Archie shrugged. "Yeah."

"Well?"

"Well, what?"

Gordon scowled. "I asked you your rank."

"You did not," Archie responded. "You asked me if I had one."

The others laughed, but the new team sergeant's expression remained stony. "You're going to find your life a hell of a lot more pleasant if you don't piss me off, Dobbs. *Now what is your rank?*"

"Sergeant E-5," Dobbs answered. "I'm the detachment recon man."

"Well, my rank is master sergeant E-8 and I'm the detachment segeant," Gordon said. "And I suggest you keep that in mind at all times. Understood?"

"Yes, Sergeant," Dobbs answered.

Gordon turned to the other new men. "Each of you stand up. Give your name, rank, former unit, and military occupational specification."

The Australian responded first. "Tom Newcomb, staff sergeant, Australian Special Air Service, infantry weapons and tactics."

Another newcomer, a short, extremely muscular Oriental stood up. When he smiled, it appeared his eyes had folded shut. "I am Chun Kim, master sergeant, South Korean Marine Corps. I work with infantry support weapons."

The third, obviously an American, stepped forward. He was a tall, extremely slim man with a shock of black hair that would have been unruly had it not been cut short to his narrow skull. "Howdy. I'm from the Navy SEALs and my name is Fred Jackson—they call me Sparks 'cause I'm a commo man."

"Chief Claud Jenkins, United States Navy Underwater Demolitions Teams," the fourth said. He was a salty-looking man with a squint. Short and heavyset with gray hair surmounting his weathered face, he appeared to be about fifteen years beyond the thirty-five his navy records showed. "I make things go boom. I've worked with the army before and they always end up calling me Popeye. So if you're so inclined, go ahead, but don't think you've come up with an original idea."

Archie Dobbs laughed. "Right, Popeye, we'll—"

"At ease!" Master Sergeant Duncan Gordon's voice exploded in the bunker. He waited for the place to quiet

down; then he turned toward the final man, an imposing little fellow. "And who are you?"

The skinny kid, looking nervous and scared, grinned weakly. "Well . . . I'm Spesh'list Orville Hanover . . . and I'm a TI&E NCO."

This time it was the black demo sergeant Calvin Culpepper who exploded into laughter. "Where you gonna set up the fuckin' TI&E board, Orville?"

"At ease!" Gordon bellowed.

Another aircraft had landed at about the same time the helicopter had arrived at the Black Eagles' base camp. The other, however, had come in at the Hanoi airport several hundred miles to the north. It was a Russion IL-14. The twin-engine prop airliner bore the markings of the Soviet airline Aeroflot.

The airplane, on a special diplomatic mission, was met without fanfare by various contingents of the North Vietnamese government. One Russian traveler, a rugged-looking individual with a light complexion and pale blue eyes, walked down the unloading ramp and strode over to a waiting, unmarked Soviet UAZ-69A command car.

His name was Gregori Krashchenko, an ex-captain of the Russian army's parachute rifle branch, he had transferred to the KGB several years previously. Now, at the age of thirty-seven, Krashchenko was a lieutenant colonel whose specialty was military intelligence — particularly regarding American forces serving in Southeast Asia. This branch of the Soviet Union's feared KGB was becoming more active as the United States activities in the area increased.

Krashchenko had been sent on a special assignment

regarding the clandestine raid on a secret prison camp in North Vietnam known as Garrison Three. Not only had a group of commandos successfully infiltrated the area and released all prisoners, but they had taken two important communist personages with them. The first was the commander of the camp, Colonel Nguyen Chi Roi, who was North Vietnam's premier interrogator of American prisoners. The second was his coach and mentor, a North Korean named Doctor Yoon Hwan. Doctor Yoon, now presumed dead, had learned the inquisition trade during the Korean War by experimenting with U.S. pilots who had been shot down. The knowledge he'd acquired and the methods he'd developed from examining American POWs had made him a most valuable asset to the spread of world socialism.

Doctor Yoon had also been greatly appreciated by the Russians because he had been a Korean working successfully with the North Vietnamese. This had been considered rather unusual since the two Oriental peoples displayed a remarkable tendency to look down their noses at each other. The Russians, an extremely racist group, considered it a duty to lead these ethnic groups, whom they considered inferior and barbaric, along the proper paths of Communism. They had serious problems in the Soviet Union with their own Tartars and Mongols, but they kept these unfortunate people under control by extreme repressions which caused these Orientals to live in a state of poverty that was appalling even by Russian standards.

The command car took Colonel Krashchenko through the city and out to an old French garrison. There, from behind the whitewashed stone of a former colonial headquarters, the North Vietnamese directed their intelligence service.

Krashchenko wasted no time with preliminaries when he met his native counterpart. This North Vietnamese was Major Truong Van. Also an intelligence officer, Truong had been assigned to assist Krashchenko — and mostly learn from him — during his stay in Southeast Asia.

The Russian insisted on getting right to work. He was quickly ushered into the special office that had been provided with extra guards along with electronic surveillance and security devices. Maps and file cabinets had been set up to facilitate the work that was to be done there.

And there were also complete reports on the Garrison Three raid and the battles that had occurred afterward waiting for him. A number of photographs of the cadavers of dead raiders that the North Vietnamese had been able to obtain were included in this special file.

"Have all these men been identified?" Krashchenko asked.

"Yes, Comrade," the North Vietnamese intelligence officer answered.

"And these are all that were killed despite the massive casualties they inflicted on the North Vietnamese units fighting them?"

The officer hung his head. "Yes, Comrade. That is, regrettably, the truth."

"I see," Krashchenko said. He went through the photographs, noting the bloody condition of the bodies, the features distorted by the violence of their deaths — each photographed by the North Vietnamese where it lay sprawled on the ground. He read each name aloud, and studied the distorted, sometimes mutilated faces, of the dead men:

Sergeant Trent Hodges
Sergeant First Class Norman Ormond
Hospital Corpsman Michael Littleton
Sergeant Demond Carter
Sergeant First Class Manuel Rivera
Sergeant Ray Limo
Sergeant First Class Jan Miskoski
Lieutenant William Thompson
First Lieutenant Richard Wakely
Staff Sergeant Marvin Dayton

The KGB man tossed the pictures back on the table in front of him. "Have the units of these dead imperialists been identified?"

"Some." Truong answered. "Thompson and Littleton were navy men belonging to the SEAL commandos. The one named Dayton had been our prisoner and was taken from Garrison Three. All we know of the others is that they were members of the American army's Special Forces. We know nothing of which particular detachment they may have been assigned to."

"It may be a unique outfit that we've yet to learn about," Krashchenko said. "You're sure this is *all* you have?"

"Yes, Comrade Colonel," the North Vietnamese officer said. "We think we killed more, but the Imperialists either buried them or took the bodies away to their own lines."

"Perhaps so," Krashchenko conceded. He lit a cigarette and looked up at the officer. "Do you know why I've been assigned here?"

"Not exactly, Comrade Colonel."

"Soviet intelligence is most curious about this group of commandos," the Russian explained. "In fact, there is such an interest in this case, that my sole duty will be to concentrate on the project. These gangsters must be identified, located and destroyed. Even if it means doing so in South Vietnam. If we must, we can send a special killer team down to do just that."

"We have patriotic raiders in the area now, Comrade Colonel," the North Vietnamese said.

"With luck, perhaps they will stumble across the bandits and eliminate them," Krashchenko said. "In the meantime, I shall stay here and wait until they either pop up again or we begin to receive information about them. At this moment, there are special agents doing nothing but trying to identify and isolate this mysterious band of marauders."

The intelligence officer grinned. "Then, without a doubt, they will soon be destroyed."

"Of course, comrade," the Soviet officer said, smiling back. "It is only a matter of time."

CHAPTER FOUR

The silence of the night ripped apart under the brilliant thunder of incoming mortar rounds.

The men in the Black Eagles bunker rolled out of their fartsacks and grabbed their weapons. Master Sergeant Gordon crawled hurriedly across the floor to Lieutenant Dinky Dow. "What's the attack SOP, sir?" he asked. The senior NCO sincerely regretted not having inquired into the matter earlier. He felt he had begun his new assignment on a bad note.

"Our area of fighting is east side of perimeter," Dinky Dow shouted as the explosions increased in intensity. "VC attack us all the same every time—mortars' then riflemen come across wire. Very crazy, very dangerous. Lot of grenades."

"Right, sir," Gordon said. "Maybe you should take overall command until I learn the ropes more."

"Sure! No problem," Dinky Dow said. "When barrage let up, we go. Horny Galchaser on guard duty at defensive position in trench."

Several more series of mortar shells struck the camp, then there was nothing but a buzzing in the punished eardrums of the men.

Dinky Dow, clad in boots and shorts and with a bandoleer of M-16 ammo slung across his shoulders, leaped up and raced out of the bunker with the others on his heels. The new men, a bit confused, stumbled after him.

The Vietnamese officer led them to a sandbagged trench. Barbed-wire entanglements stretched out from the defensive position for a space of fifty yards.

Horny Galchaser met Dinky Dow and Gordon as they entered the trench. "Most of the obstacle's been blown up by the shelling," he told them. "So have the mines and booby traps planted in and around the strands."

The attack had opened up the area for the enemy infantry which now wiggled toward them in the darkness.

From somewhere in the center of the camp, an 81-mm mortar barked and sent a round high in the air. It was a flare, and burst in the sky with a brilliance that made it suddenly seem like day.

The defenders could see the black-clad VC clearly. They opened fire and the enemy responded with their supporting automatic weapons as the attack groups continued closing in. Now and then one of the figures would leap or roll over under the shock of a well-aimed bullet.

Then it was dark again.

"Goddamn it!" Calvin Culpepper swore. "I wish that fuckin' mortar crew would keep at least one flare in the air at all times."

As if in response to his demands, the scene was lit up by a fresh illuminating round. Liam O'Quinn took advantage of the light to rush from man to man handing out a pair of M-26 grenades to each member of the detachment.

"Ain't the M-79s in yet?" Horny Galchaser asked the marine sergeant as he took the deadly egg-shaped devices. He referred to a type of grenade launcher that had been on requisition for several weeks.

"Am I shootin' one o' the sonofabitches at them Charlies out there?" Lightfingers O'Quinn demanded.

"Well . . . no, you ain't," Galchaser said.

"Then I ain't been able to draw the fuckin' thing yet," Lightfingers growled as he hurried away to continue passing out the M-26s.

Orville Hanover, wide-eyed and astounded, held onto his M-16 rifle and stared in wonder at the sight of the attackers before him.

"Say, buddy," Archie Dobbs, beside him, remarked. "Don't you think it would be a good idea to fire at them bastards? In case you ain't noticed, they're assaulting our position."

"Jesus! Jesus!" Orville exclaimed. He looked down at the M-16. "I don't know how to shoot this thing. I had an M-14 back at Fort Dix and I only took it out of the arms room for parades. I ain't fired a weapon since basic."

"Watch me," Archie told him. He took Orville's weapon and crammed a magazine into it. Then he snapped the charging handle and handed it back. "I got it set on semiauto," he said. "Did you see how I did that?"

"Yeah," Orville answered. His training with the other model weapon had been enough to give him an understanding of this different one. He swallowed hard and shoved the muzzle over the sandbags in front of him.

The initial wave of the enemy had been shot down, but a more numerous second group now pressed forward over their bodies. Many of these, naked and shrieking in rage, appeared to be under the influence of more than just zeal for their cause. A closer physical examination would have revealed the dilated eyes and dry mouths of people under the influence of heavy doses of powerful narcotics.

All the Black Eagles, including Orville now, fired rapidly at targets of opportunity within their individual fire zones. Now the flares floated continuously above them, and the other mortars added high explosive rounds on predetermined areas.

But they were a minute or so too slow.

The screaming enemy leaped over the last remnants of the ruined wire and charged the trench. Despite their rapid firing, the Black Eagles could not stop the assault. Each of the old hands, knowing the drill, tossed one of the grenades into the midst of the Viet Cong.

Screams and gasps of pain followed the explosions as parts of bodies flew through the air. But the survivors, moving among the mangled, torn cadavers of their comrades, were now only fifteen yards away. These were suicide troops, hopped up and prepared to die. Dinky Dow picked out a particularly vocal one and squeezed off three quick rounds. The VC jerked and danced under the impact of the slugs before toppling to the ground.

Another came in behind his comrade and leaped through the air at the trench. The Australian Newcomb fired a split second too quick and missed. Momentum carried the attacker into the trench to collide with the SAS man, slamming him against the opposite earthen wall. Newcomb's M-16 was knocked from his hands, but his instincts came into play and he was not even aware he had drawn the dagger carried in the scabbard strapped to his boot. The blade, kept razor sharp, slashed across the VC's throat in both forehand and backhand strokes. Then Newcomb drove it into the man's abdomen and up under his ribs.

The Communist guerrilla gasped and tried a horizontal butt stroke with his AK-47, but had neither the room nor the strength to do more serious damage than inflict a cut on the Australian's temple. Newcomb thrust the knife three more times until his opponent collapsed at his feet.

Then it was quiet.

A few figures stirred outside the trench system and moans could be heard.

"Okay. They finished," Dinky Dow said.

"Are you sure, sir?" Gordon asked.

"You bet! VC go home. But mortars first. Get down!"

Everybody ducked down into the trench at the same moment the incoming rounds of this fresh barrage exploded around them.

Dinky Dow nudged Gordon and explained the situation by shouting in his ear. "VC keep us from chasing them. Also kill all their wounded they no take with them, see?"

Gordon nodded his understanding as they endured fifteen minutes of incoming rounds before the battle ended. When it was quiet again, the NCO stood up. "What the hell happened to our counter-battery fire?"

"The heavy weapons unit here is ARVN, Sergeant," Horny Galchaser explained to him. "Not too swift, I'm afraid. But we're not hit that often, so I suppose it doesn't matter much."

"What kind of attack was that?" Gordon demanded. "What did they expect to gain from it?"

Archie Dobbs wiped the prespiration from his face. "Only to let us know they're out there and can raid us whenever they want."

"Why don't we go out and hit them?" Gordon asked.

"Where?" Dobbs answered with his own question.

"They melt back into the jungle and the population. This area is ours in the daytime, but their's at night."

Gordon spat. "Fucked up war."

"I think that's the way it'll be written in the history books," Dobbs said. He turned to Orville Hanover. "How'd you do, kid?"

Orville shrugged. "I shot at 'em, but I don't know if I got any or not."

"You'll do better the next time," Archie said.

"Next time?" Orville wailed. "I only got eight months left in the army."

Archie grinned at him. "From all indications, it's gonna be the most exciting time of your military career."

"I just hope I survive it," Orville said. "And I wish somebody'd tell me what the hell I'm doing over here."

"Saving the world from Communism, young man," Archie said. "C'mon, I'll buy you a cup o' C-ration coffee."

Master Sergeant Gordon's voice interrupted the small talk of the detachment. "You people pull those magazines out of your weapons and crank those charging handles. Then put on the safeties. I don't want any accidental shooting."

He watched as the men complied; then he positioned himself at the trench exit to personally check every weapon before allowing the troops to return to their quarters.

Master Sergeant Duncan Gordon, from Binghamton, New York, had been in the army for seventeen years. He had enlisted as an eager eighteen-year-old, just missing World War II. Gordon had volunteered to be a paratrooper to make up for this lack of combat opportunity. Eventually assigned to the 187th Airborne

Regimental Combat Team in Japan, his desire to see action was surprisingly fulfilled by North Korea's cowardly and infamous attack across the 38th parallel in June of 1950.

Gordon saw plenty of combat duty with his outfit in that conflict, earning a silver star and two purple hearts.

After Korea he had served with various other airborne units, maturing and further adapting himself to military life within the spit-and-polish environments. But this devotion to duty eventually cost him dearly in his personal life.

Gordon had married his hometown sweetheart after the Korean War, but the young woman could not abide the life of an army wife. The marriage lasted three years, produced no children, and was terminated without any protest from Gordon. He simply turned back to the military life and devoted himself completely and wholly to its demands.

When he volunteered for Special Forces, he had done it in order to make himself a more rounded professional soldier. With only a year as a Green Beret, Duncan still had many things to learn about unconventional warfare — and the type of men who participated in it.

Now he glanced out at the blown-up wire for a final look at the battle scene. Then he turned and started back for the Black Eagles' bunker. He wanted to talk to the men about wearing complete uniforms during duty hours. There was no reason for them to be hatless and shirtless so much of the time.

CHAPTER FIVE

Captain Falconi slipped his legs over the side of the jeep and pushed himself out of the vehicle. He strolled up to the MP at the gate in the barbed-wire fence and presented his ID card. A quick phone call to verify his identification resulted in the officer being allowed to enter the compound.

He walked across an open space to the entrance of the building that housed the headquarters of SOG, Special Operations Group, at Peterson Field across Saigon from the sprawling Tan Son Nhut air base.

Another guard also carefully checked him out before allowing the officer to enter the foyer of the building. Once inside he had to wait for an escort to take him up to his final destination—the office of a senior CIA operative named Chuck Fagin.

Captain Robert Mikhailovich Falconi was the commanding officer of the Black Eagles. Detached from the U.S. Army's crack 5th Special Forces group to lead the special unit, Falconi was a superprofessional in unconventional warfare. Trained and experienced in both insurgency and counterinsurgency, he was an expert in weapons as complicated as laser-directed antitank missiles as well as other deadly playthings more simple and direct, such as crossbows or knives. His hands, too, were dangerous. An accomplished and skillful martial artist,

Robert Falconi was unabashedly patriotic and violently anti-Communist.

He picked up the former traits from his father, a career army man, whose profession had given his son the opportunity to be raised as an army brat on various military posts not only throughout the States but in Japan and Europe as well. Falconi's hatred of Communist totalitarianism had been passed to him by his mother, a Russian Jew whose family had been murdered as a result of Joseph Stalin's anti-Semitic policies and his persecutions of her poeple.

A strict noncomformist, any conflict his flamboyant personality created with his devotion to the army or with the restrictions of the military community was tempered somewhat by Falconi through serving in Special Forces where both men and officers were expected to be individualistic and self-reliant. His assignment as commanding officer of the Black Eagles and his subsequent placement directly under the supervision of CIA case officers had increased the need for his peculiar talents in leadership and combat.

"Captain Falconi?"

He turned and faced the MP sergeant. "Right."

"I'm your escort, sir. Follow me, please."

No one—absolutely *no one*—was allowed to wander alone through SOG headquarters unless properly authorized. Even Robert Falconi didn't have that right.

The sergeant led him up to the third floor and down a dimly lit hall. The air conditioning didn't work quite so well up that high in the building, and it was a bit stuffy. They stopped in front of a door. The sergeant knocked, opened the heavy portal, and then stood back respectfully.

Falconi stepped into the outer office. He smiled at the beautiful young Eurasian woman seated at the desk there. Lean, yet shapely, her hair was a glossy black and her almond-shaped eyes a dark brown. Her features displayed the best combination of her European and Oriental bloodlines. She wore the uniform of a South Vietnamese army major.

Andrea Thuy, half Vietnamese, half French — and all woman — hated Communists with even more intensity than did Robert Falconi. After her parents were murdered by the Red Viet Minh, she had been placed in an orphanage and raised by Catholic nuns. When the Pathet Lao attacked the religious mission, they murdered the nuns and made the older girls prisoners.

The Red fanatics amused themsleves by brutally and repeatedly raping the young women they held prisoner. Andrea was one of those forced to suffer this degrading mistreatment.

She endured this horror until the carelessness of the guards gave her an opportunity to escape during one of the many seesaw battles that constantly broke out in the area. Andrea joined a group of refugees heading south, going with them until they met up with South Vietnamese army troops.

Like all such displaced persons, Andrea was subjected to an intelligence interrogation which revealed her background and hatred for the Communist enemy. The anti-Red factions found her a willing and able volunteer to work in their efforts against the enemy to the north.

The South Vietnamese government employed her on clandestine missions from time to time. Fluent in French, Vietnamese, and Laotian, they further schooled her in English and several Southeast Asian dialects and gave her a thorough training as an intelligence operative. She had even worked one mission with the Black Eagles—Operation Hanoi Hellground. Andrea now spent most of her time as an intelligence and operations advisor and an aide to Chuck Fagin, the CIA officer recently assigned to the Black Eagles.

Andrea greeted Robert Falconi with more than just a warm smile. She came around her desk, embraced him tightly, and then kissed the American officer warmly on the lips. They had become lovers, but only in the strange way of people locked tightly into a cause and mission. Furtive and brief encounters between them were meaningful and fulfilling, yet both were willing to endure long separations as they fought the good war against the people they hated the most.

"Robert," Andrea said breaking off their kiss. "I've not seen you since the Black Eagles' last operation. Why haven't you been to Saigon?"

"That most certainly was not my idea," Robert Falconi said. "We were taken to our new base camp out in the boonies right after Operation Song Bo Slaughter. Then SOG involved me in a long debriefing, plus the interrogation of Colonel Nguyen."

She smiled. "I saw the paperwork. You had a bit of explaining to do about Doctor Yoon Hwan too."

"I sure as hell did," Falconi agreed. Then he shrugged. "But who can blame the brass? When you're supposed to bring a prisoner out with you and end up beating the hell out of him just before one of your officers shoots him, your bosses naturally tend to get a bit testy about it."

"I noticed you were glib enough to avoid trouble,"

Andrea said. "Have you met the new case officer?"

"No," Falconi answered. "I only recently heard that Clayton had been transferred. I'll miss him. How's the new guy?"

"Just your type," Andrea said. "Come on. I'll introduce you. He's been on a trip to the States." She took Falconi's hand and led him over to a door. She rapped on it.

"Yeah, Andrea. C'mon in." The voice was gruff but had a friendly ring to it.

The woman opened the door and preceded Falconi into the office. "This is the man you've been expecting. Captain Robert Falconi. Robert, this is Chuck Fagin."

Falconi walked up to his desk and shook hands. "Glad to know you, Mister Fagin."

"I prefer Chuck," Fagin said. "And I'm glad to finally meet you, Bob . . . or, should I say Falcon? That's what I hear they call you."

"Right."

"Fine, Falcon. Sit down," Fagin said. "I've been up to my ears in preparatory work the past three weeks, traveling all over hell and back to set up this coming mission."

"I presume I'm here for the preliminary briefing," Falconi said settling down in a worn, leather chair in front of Fagin's desk.

"Right. Andrea will take care of explaining the operation," Fagin said. "The information I have for you involves your infiltration and exfiltration. That's what I've seen setting up."

"Sure." Falconi turned to Andrea. "So what's our job this trip?"

"You will be going into Laos," Andrea said. "To destroy the site of a nuclear power plant."

Falconi was quiet for a few incredulous seconds. "Are you telling me that there is one of those setups in Laos."

Andrea shook her head. "It's not built yet, but the preliminary construction has begun. Your mission will be to bring it down around their ears."

"Why not wait until they build it?"

Fagin interrupted. "That's the last goddamned thing we want the Reds to construct here in Southeast Asia."

"Then what good will it do simply to knock down the structures they've constructed during the primary stages?" Falconi asked.

"Because it will show them we know all about their insidious little project," Fagin answered. "The fact we were able to come up with that intelligence will convince the Communists that even if they do construct one we will find out about it eventually and destroy it. At least in this part of the world. And they won't want a damaged, malfunctioning, leaking nuclear facility in their midst."

"That makes sense," Falconi said.

Andrea's face bore a serious expression. "The reactor they plan on having there is not a standard model, Robert. It is a Fermi breeder—the most dangerous kind. It produces more radioactive material—that is, uranium or plutonium."

"I see," Falconi said. "That does sound bad."

"And that's not all," Fagin added. "The Fermi is less stable than other reactors. And, worse yet, most use mercury fulmite for a coolant. This is more effective than water, but it is unstable and highly toxic. It can cause genetic deformities."

"I'm sorry," Falconi said. "But I'm not up to date on all

this nuclear stuff. Despite your explanations, I don't completely understand what we're dealing with here."

"Let me fill you in a bit on Fermi breeders, Falcon," Andrea said. "This is how they work. The core is energized uranium. A blanket of decayed neptunium is placed around the core before the atom-smashing process is begun. That's done by inserting baron rods into the reactor core."

Falconi sighed. "I still don't follow everything you're saying, but keep it up and I'll do my best."

"Okay," Andrea said. "Energized atoms will burst from the core into the neptunium which is then changed into plutonium. And plutonium also has the most dangerous forms of radiation poisons, not to mention that it takes less than five pounds of the stuff to make an Atomic bomb."

"Jesus!" Falconi exclaimed.

Andrea spoke with dread in her voice. "Can you imagine such power available to fanatics like the Pathet Lao?"

"The Black Eagles will never have a mission more important than this one," Fagin said.

"I guess not," Falconi agreed.

"You people are going to have to really be up for this undertaking," Andrea told him. "The old sweats— Dobbs, Galchaser, Culpepper, O'Quinn, McCorckel, and Dinky Dow—are ready to go. I'm not acquainted with the new replacements for the men lost in the last operation."

"I've only met the new team sergeant," Falconi said. "His name is Duncan Gordon, an E-8, who seems somewhat of a stuffed shirt. A lot of years of service in airborne units, but he hasn't been in SF for much more

43

than a year. I hope he didn't bring a spit-and-polish attitude with him."

"You sound worried," Fagin said.

"I am. I had a chance to have only a short conversation with him before he flew out to the base camp with the replacements. During those few moments I tried to impress on him that he'd have a tough row to hoe under the best of circumstances," Falconi explained. "Anybody taking Top's place is going to meet a lot of resentment. From the way Gordon talked, he seemed to think it didn't matter. He even came up with that old cliché about not giving a damn about winning popularity contests."

"That could make the mission a hell of a lot rougher," Fagin said.

"It might even spell the difference between success and failure," Andrea suggested solemnly.

"If this mission falls through," Fagin said in a cold voice, "then the gaddamned Reds are not only going to construct that one breeder, they'll put 'em in all over the place."

"You're right," Falconi said. "By the way, how're we going in on this? Parachute infiltration?"

"Nope," Fagin said. "You'll be going in by glider."

"Beg pardon?"

"Glider . . . you're going into the operational area in a glider," Fagin repeated.

"Then how the hell are we getting out of there?" Falconi asked.

"Same way."

"Oh. A powered one, hey?"

"Nope. You'll be infiltrated and exfiltrated in a remake of a World War II model Waco CG-

44

A," Fagin said.

Falconi leaned forward in the chair. "I don't know diddly squat about gliders, I admit. But I do know the damn things have to be towed, and that they don't take off on their own."

"Right."

"Sounds like getting us out is pretty low in the priorities of this mission," Falconi remarked coldly.

Fagin smiled. "Why don't we let Andrea continue with the briefing?"

CHAPTER SIX

The high-pitched blast of noise that unexpectedl'
erupted outside the bunker made Archie Dobbs jump.
"What the hell was that?"

"Christ!" Malpractice McCorckel said. "It was a thun
der whistle."

"I ain't heard one o' them since boot camp," Light
fingers O'Quinn remarked. "Who's blowin' the fuckin
thing?"

Calvin Culpepper glanced out the bunker's forward
firing slit, then groaned, "Oh, shit!"

"What's 'a matter, Calvin?" Dobbs asked.

"It's Sergeant Gordon."

The device shrilled again. This time the new team
sergeant added his voice to the noise. "Outside, Black
Eagles! Fall outside on the double!"

Tom Newcomb the Australian was surprised. "I didn'
know you blokes used them things in this sort of an out
fit."

"What the hell!" Horny Galchaser exclaimed. "Mus
be somethin' big. Let's go, guys!"

The eleven men — army, navy, and marine — climbed
out of the bunker entrance and gathered around
Gordon. He frowned at them. "Fall in!"

They formed up haphazardly. "What's goin' on?"
Archie Dobbs asked.

"At ease! Dress to the right," Gordon ordered them. "You've all been in the army long enough to know how to fall in properly, haven't you?"

"Hell!" Lightfingers O'Quinn remarked caustically. "I ain't *never* been in the army."

Gordon glared at him. "You'll find it a distinct disadvantage to be a wise-ass whether you have or not!"

Orville Hanover, his attitude now confused and his feelings torn between a desire for his former soft job and an appreciation of the apparent lack of discipline in this crazy new situation into which the army had thrust him, didn't quite know how to react to the situation.

Dobbs scowled. "Did you blow that fuckin' whistle just to get us outside."

Gordon took three long strides toward him until he stood nose to nose with Dobbs. "Do you understand *at ease?*"

"Do you understand *cram it?*" Dobbs retorted.

Master Sergeant Gordon's face reddened with anger and he stepped back. "I'll deal with you later, Dobbs." He surveyed the group. All were shirtless and only Malpractice and Horny wore headgear — different types however — while Dobbs was standing in his shower shoes. "You will all return to the bunker and, at the sound of my whistle, fall back outside in proper uniform. That includes fatigue jackets, caps, and boots. Now — fall *out!*"

The Black Eagles retraced their steps, returning to the bunker interior. As they dressed Archie Dobbs gritted his teeth in anger. "Who the fuck does he think he is, huh? Chickenshit sonofabitch comin' in here thinkin' he's gonna take Top's place."

"Shit!" Calvin swore, his black face displaying the

anger he felt. "Gordon figures he *is* the Top."

"I'll never call him that," Horny said.

"Right!" Lightfingers echoed. "There ain't no way in hell he's ever gonna be the Top. The sonofabitch must think he's runnin' recruits through AIT in the 82nd Airborne Division."

Newcomb and the Korean marine, Chun, were both unsure as to who was correct. Their exposure to the American armed forces was limited, and this situation did very little to clear up any questions they might have as to the proper protocol to observe.

The whistle shrilled loudly, and the detachment again went outside. This time, in full uniform, they fell in properly facing the detachment's top NCO.

"Stand at ease," Gordon told them. "We have a special detail to tend to. An aircarft is coming in here with some equipment for us."

"I don't know nothin' about any equipment," Lightfingers O'Quinn protested.

"Does *at ease* in the Marine Corps mean the same as it does in the army?" Gordon asked. But before Lightfingers could answer, he continued. "In the army it means, *quiet, shut up, don't talk,* or *silence!* You take your pick, but you obey that order to be *at ease!*"

Lightfingers glared in sullen anger at the more senior noncommissioned officer. "I'm the supply NCO for the detachment, so I got the responsibility for all equipment matters involving the outfit."

Gordon spoke in a cold voice. "And I'm the detachment sergeant. I'll decide what information gets passed down the chain of command."

Lightfingers gritted his teeth. "Yes, Sergeant."

"Now," Gordon said. "As I was saying: we have been

tasked to unload an incoming aircraft that is bringing us some special equipment. We are going to march over to the landing strip in a military manner and await its arrival. Understood?"

The group was silent.

"I asked you if you understood me? Now — *do you understand*?"

"Yes, Sergeant," they answered in unison.

"Good. Detail, ten-*hut*! Right, *face*! For'd, *march*!"

The group, with Gordon counting cadence, marched through the astounded Special Forces troopers as they crossed the camp. The other members of the garrison looked up from their various tasks at the unusual sight of a formation of men in step with an NCO counting cadence.

One trooper stopped in the middle of his task involving the careful packing of a demolitions kit. "Hey," he hollered out at the marching men, "is there a division parade laid on?"

Another Special Forces man nearby cackled loudly. "Road guards out! Road guards out!" he yelled. His companion, standing nearby, pulled a harmonica from his pocket and began a loud rendition of *The Stars and Stripes Forever* while the Black Eagles seethed under the taunts.

When the detachment reached the air strip, they were halted. After warning them not to leave the area, the master sergeant allowed them to break formation and wait for the expected airplane to arrive.

Major Truong Van hurried down the hall with the dispatch in his hand. He went into the office recently assigned to him and the Russian KGB colonel Gregori

Krashchenko.

"Comrade Colonel," Truong cried triumphantly. "We have a list of American army officers detached from their units in South Vietnam."

"Good," the Russian said. "One or more of them must be assigned to Commando X."

Krashchenko, because he had no proper unit designation for the raiding unit that had twice penetrated the Communist lines, had decided to refer to it as Commando X until it was correctly identified.

The KGB colonel took the list and scanned it. "Ah! There are several who can be eliminated quickly from our roster of potential bandits. Do you see which ones, Comrade Major Truong?"

"Yes," Truong answered. "The quartermaster corps and transportation officers listed here certainly are not serving in such capacities as raiders and saboteurs."

"Exactly," Krashchenko said. "But we have several paratroop and infantry leaders who could well be part of such a group."

"This is all painstaking detective work, Comrade," Truong commented.

"Yes," Krashchenko agreed. "But once we identify enough of these gangsters, then our agents in the south can use the contacts and methods they've developed to pinpoint the location of this unit."

"And when we know that, we will have no trouble destroying them. I suggest a suicide squad with explosives attached to them. They could infiltrate Commando X's position as human bombs and then destroy the unit," Truong said. "But who can supply us with the positive identification we shall need?"

"My comrades in the KGB," Krashchenko answered.

"They will run these individuals' names through our computer and obtain much valuable information."

"Then your organization maintains an extensive file on many Americans, correct, Comrade Colonel Krashchenko?"

"Exactly," the Russian said. "Now let's see who the potential members of Commando X are . . . Albertson, 1st Cavalry . . . Barker, 174th Airborne . . . Donaldson, 5th Special Forces . . . Edelmann, 1st Cavalry . . . Erickson, 1st Division . . . Falconi, 5th Special Forces . . . Fenster, 174th Airbone . . ."

The "control tower" at the B-Team base camp was no more than a small bunker. With only a radio inside, the air traffic control job consisted of little more than to inform any incoming aircraft that it was either safe or unsafe to land—both conditions depending on the proximity and activities of the local Viet Cong.

Sometimes, however, aircrews found it unnecessary to inquire about conditions when they preceived geysers of earth and fire erupting from mortar explosions across the airstrip.

That particular day it was safe.

The C-130 Hercules transport banked gracefully over the far hills and slowly turned onto the approach path to the crude runway. The pilot had flown in there many times, and the landing of his plane showed it. Confidently and serenely the big aircarft sank until the wheels contacted the hard-packed dirt, sending swirls of dust flying up in the prop blast behind the big flying machine.

The Black Eagles, under Master Sergeant Gordon's stern gaze, waited until the C-130 taxied up to where they waited by the base off-loading area. The plane slowly turned around and the engines were cut. At the same time a ground crew scurried forward with wheel chocks. A sudden grinding noise revealed that the big tailgate of the aircraft was being lowered to allow access to the fuselage interior.

When the ramp was all the way down, Captain Falconi walked down it with a duffel bag over his left shoulder and an oversized briefcase in his right hand. He grinned at his men. "Hey, big team," he called out. "How goes it?"

"Do I have an earful for you, Falcon," Archie Dobbs growled.

Gordon snapped to attention and saluted. "Sir, Sergeant Gordon, detachment sergeant, reporting to the commanding officer."

Falcon sat the briefcase down and returned the salute. "How've you been, Sergeant Gordon?"

"Fine, sir. The men are here to unload the new gear."

Orville Hanover, with a pilot's curiosity, eased over to look up into the big C-130. He saw another man unstrapping himself from the web seats inside the fuselage. The stranger wore an unmarked fatigue uniform and seemed very interested in the condition of the single, extremely large crate lashed to the deck of the plane. When he walked toward the open ramp during his brief inspection, Orville gasped aloud.

"J.T.! J. T. Beamer!"

Beamer turned at the sound of his name and stared disbelievingly at the small slim figure standing out on the airstrip.

"Is that you, Orville?" he asked.

"Sure is," Orville answered. "What in the world are

you doing in this neck of the woods?"

"I might ask you the same," J.T. said trotting down the ramp. "Except you're probably in the same boat I am — got to keep your mouth closed, right?"

Orville emitted a nervous laugh. "Hell! I don't know a damned thing." He shook hands with his friend. "I heard you were in jail in Texas."

"Yeah, got caught with a joint during a visit to Dallas," J.T. explained. "But I got pardoned and I've been at McChord Air Force Base in Washington working on a special project. See that crate there? Well, it's—"

Master Sergeant Gordon's loud voice interrupted them. "Knock off the bullshit!" He turned toward the other Black Eagles. "Let's go, people! Unlash the crate and wheel her out."

"What's in that big box anyhow?" Orville asked.

"Something I figure has a lot to do with you, ol' buddy," J.T. answered. "A glider."

"You two!" Gordon snapped at them. "I told you to be at ease. Get your asses in gear and lend a hand here. You can renew your friendship with all the kisses and hugs you want to later. And there'll be a briefing to answer any questions you have. Move it!"

The two friends went up the ramp together. Orville shook his head in befuddled curiosity. "Now why would anybody want to sailplane in Vietnam?"

"That ain't no sailplane, buddy," J.T. corrected him. "It's a glider. So if you're the guy they've picked to pilot it, don't bother searching out any thermals. The best you'll be able to do is maintain the heading while she sinks through the air — fast!"

"You mean a controlled descent?" Orville asked.

"It'll be *controlled* if you're lucky," J.T. remarked.

"What's the glide ratio?" Orville asked with some mis-givings.

"On paper it looks like about one-to-fifteen," J.T. an-swered. He glanced around at the sky. "But it's hard to tell in this heavy humidity . . . and, particularly, if it's flown at night."

"*Night!*" Orville exclaimed.

"Yeah," J.T. said with a weak grin. "In the absolute blackest conditions you can see."

"What kind of instruments are in that thing?" Orville inquired as he grew more worried.

"Nothing that'll help you with blind flying."

Orville stopped in midstride. Suddenly recalling his conversation with the civilian in Fort Dix about his pi-loting experiences, the young soldier uttered the expres-sion he had been using quite a bit since that day.

"Oh, shit!"

CHAPTER SEVEN

The immediate three-day period after Falconi's arrival with the glider had been a busy and productive one for the Black Eagles.

The aircraft, still stored away in its wooden box, had been set by the side of the airstrip. Covered with tarpaulins and sandbags — the former to keep out the weather; the latter to block any flying shrapnel during potential attacks — the motorless flying machine awaited the attention it would get at the proper moment.

Meanwhile, the Black Eagles' bunker had been put off limits from the rest of the base by guards provided from the garrison. These armed troopers made sure no one approached within twenty-five meters of the place. This was normal procedure for any unit going through the phase of their mission called isolation. It was during this time that all the information on upcoming operations was dispensed.

Absolute secrecy was a must.

The fourteen men inside their sandbagged quarters poured over the documents that their leader had brought with him. Operations plans, maps, aerial photographs and other data were perused, digested, redigested, memorized, and probed for long hours.

Finally, almost seventy-two hours to the minute from his arrival, the Falcon called his flock together for the preliminary task that occurred before each and every mission—the briefing. It would be a meeting in which each man, now completely steeped in those phases of the operation pertaining to his particular skills, would enlighten his comrades regarding the dangerous activities they were about to participate in.

They gathered in the main area of the bunker which now had been arranged to facilitate the task ahead of them. Captain Falconi was the first to take the floor.

"Gentlemen," he began, "I will not mince words. Our mission in this next operation is to infiltrate into Laos, locate the construction site of a nuclear breeder reactor, and destroy it with demolitions. We will then exfiltrate back to this very camp in which we sit."

"You mean that's a real live nuclear plant we're hitting?" Horny Galchaser asked.

"No," Falconi answered. "Let me emphasize that it's only one that is being built at this moment. The reason for our mission is to show the Reds the uselessness of constructing such a facility. The detachment sergeant will now enlighten you on the execution phase of the plan." He turned to the senior NCO. "The floor is yours, Sergeant."

"Thank you, sir." Duncan Gordon, complete with collapsible pointer, stepped in front of a large map of Laos. "The target is here, men," he said. "In northern Laos at almost the exact spot of nineteen degrees latitude and one hundred and three degrees longitude. That puts us forty-four kilometers southeast of Xiangkhoang and forty kilometers due west of Highway Four. Another reference point is forty-eight kilometers south of the junction of Highways Seven and Four."

He paused to let the men locate the exact position on

their individual maps.

"Infiltration will be by glider—as you all know by now—at night. The LZ is here on the map less than a klick south, just off the ridge line indicated here. The landing will be at night with the ground crew using infrared light while our flight crew utilizes a metascope that will enable them to see the illumination that will guide the aircraft into the proper landing area."

Calvin Culpepper held up his hand. "Sergeant Gordon, how come we're using a glider? Why not parachute in?"

"The area is heavily infested with Pathet Lao troops," Gordon answered. "Any aircraft flying overhead would immediately alarm them as to the threat to the nuclear plant site. By using a glider, we can be released in the air far enough away to make a silent entry and landing. And doing this at night will also assure us that the enemy is not observing our arrival."

"Wonderful," Archie Dobbs cracked. "How the hell do we get outta there then? That glider can get in, but it sure as hell can't fly out without an airplane to tow it. Do we walk out?"

"No," Gordon responded. "We go *in* by glider, and we come *out* by glider."

"Wait a minute, Sergeant Gordon," Malpractice McCorckel protested. "After our raid, the Pathet Lao will be mad as hell and swarming all over the place! How is the plane gonna have the time to land and pick up a glider in the middle of all them bad guys?"

"By the use of a modified and enlarged glider extraction device that's been improvised by our CIA case officer Chuck Fagin. It's based on a design used in World War II for similar retrievals. It will consist of an antenna over which a trilooped, nylon tow rope will be positioned. The plane, with extracting hook extended, will come in low and snag the tow rope, pulling the motorless aircraft into the air. Then they'll haul us straight back to the airstrip of this base camp."

Horny Galchaser nodded his understanding. "Then the glider will be secured and camouflaged during the operation, right?"

Captain Falconi entered the conversation. "Exactly. The flight crew, J.T. Beamer and Orville Hanover, will remain with the aircraft as security during the operation. When we are ready to get out of there, we'll coordinate it with the retrieving ship, set it all up . . . and wait."

"I don't like that last part — waiting," Archie said with a soft moan.

"To continue," Master Sergeant Gordon announced. "Our time table on D-day, which is day after tomorrow, is as follows: On D-day — 2330 hours, formation and inspection of equipment; station time aboard the glider at 2330 hours; and we take off at 2400 hours exactly. We should be released from tow and go into the LZ at approximately 0200 hours. The landing zone will be under the control of 5th Special Forces personnel and their guerrillas. By 0400 we will be in the attack position and at 0530 launch the assault and demo operation which will take less than an hour. By 0630 at the latest we will be on our way back to the LZ for extraction at 0700 hours. After this briefing you will be divided into teams and at that point, each particular unit will be given its role in the mission. Any questions?"

"What sort of aircraft is going to tow us, Sergeant Gordon?" Tom Newcomb asked.

"A C-123," Gordon answered. "If there are no more questions, I will turn you over to Sergeant Galchaser for the intelligence phase of the briefing."

Horny Galchaser set up an enlarged aerial photo of the operational area on an easel in front of the group. "This is the place, guys, just where it was pointed out to you. The friendlies in the area, who are going to help us, are a guerrilla band of locals working with an A team out of the 5th as Sergeant Gordon mentioned. They're reliable and good despite being outnumbered and out-gunned in their own backyard. Things look okay from that standpoint. The bad guys are all over the place and there are plenty of 'em, that's why this silent entry is so important. You can expect light resistance during the first moments of the attack. This will increase gradually during the execution phase as enemy reinforcements come in from the surrounding area. That is why speed is of the essence. The local guys will keep the way clear for us back to the LZ, but *we gotta be fast!* The Pathet Lao are numerous and concentrated there, so they can only keep them off our backs for a short time. So, whatever your individual and team job is, do it fast! I'll let Lightfingers take over now for the supply part of the briefing."

The marine staff sergeant, his facial expression as surly as ever, went to the front of the room. He held up an M-79 grenade launcher. "As of now we have two of these and plenty of ammo," he said. "A grenadier will be chosen for each fire team. These are our only fire-support weapons, you guys, so let's keep that in mind. There will be no other special equipment except for demo stuff, but Calvin will tell you about that. I want each man to carry a complete — I say again, *complete* — patrol harness. That includes entrenching tools. Remember what happened during the last operation when we didn't have enough for ever'body to dig a shelter when them Migs strafed us."

"What about ponchos?" Horny Galchaser asked. "Do we bring them too?"

"Yeah. You're gonna be inspected," Lightfingers said. "So don't figure you'll be going in with any less than anybody else. The ammo issue will be standard with the grenadiers totin' additional rounds for the M-79s. Each man will get one day's C rations. That's in case things get fucked up or delayed. And I recommend some extra goodies in case we end up in a situation like in Operation Song Bo Slaughter. Remember — if the situation goes to hell, we're gonna find ourselves the center of attention in a royal cluster fuck. Expect the worst, be ready for it, and when it happens, you won't be standing there looking stupid. Any questions? Then I'll let Calvin take over."

The black demolitions sergeant went to a spot at the head of the detachment. "According to the aerial photos, the construction has just got started with a few cement pillars poured and standing — six to be exact. So we'll be taking in half-dozen forty-pound cratering charges. That means all personnel will have to be at least three hundred and eleven meters away at the time of detonation . . . unless you can get behind something substantial."

"Who's carrying the demo in?"

"Me and Popeye Jenkins will carry the main stuff, but the rest will have to be divided up among the fire teams until we're in the target area," Calvin said. "We'll work that out after you guys are broken down into teams. Now Sparks Jackson will give out the dope on commo."

The navy SEAL man had been standing off to the side of the room. Rather than go to the front, he remained where he was. "Ain't much to say," he drawled in his Arkansas accent. "We'll have two radios with us, one will be on my back and the other in the glider. They're AN/PRC-41s and we'll be using a frequency of 325 and the glider call sign will be Black Eagle. Mine will be Falcon and the LZ is Bird's Nest. The tow aircraft will be called Mother Bird." There was a groan from his audience, and he grinned. "Hell, that wasn't my idea. It was in the op plan. The commo angle is purty cut an' dried, so that's it. I'll turn you over to Malpractice McCorckel for the medical briefing."

The Special Forces medic went to the front of the room. "Evacuation of casualties will be as per SOP, 'cept we ain't taking any stretchers in with us. That's one other good reason to have them ponchos on your patrol harness. You catch one, and we'll be toting you out on that thing. If you've left it behind, I'll personally drag your bleeding carcass outta there by the heels. You are familiar with the snakes and insects there and which ones to avoid. Same for the plants. If you don't know what it is, for God's sake, don't put the fucking thing in your mouth, okay? We won't be in the operational area long, but I recommend foot powder and salt tablets. Any questions?"

Archie Dobbs raised his hand. "What if we catch the clap out there?"

Malpractice grinned at the poor humor. "Archie, we're gonna be on the ground about two and a half hours. I suppose if anyone's capable of getting clapped up during that time, it's you. My advice is to avoid contact with any indigenous female personnel."

Horny Galchaser chuckled. "I'd avoid contact with *any* female that would have anything to do with Archie."

"That's excellent counseling," Malpractice said. "If there're no more stupid questions or comments, I'll turn the briefing over to J.T. Beamer, who is going to explain our mode of transportation to us."

Beamer, feeling a bit shy in front of the strangers, went to the front of the room. "They told me I should let y'all know about my qualifications since I built that glider you're goin' in. I design sailplanes for a livin' — not much o' one, I'll admit, but what I lack in money, I make up in personal satisfaction and a few trophies when my aircraft win contests."

The men in the room, with no knowledge whatsoever of powerless craft, leaned forward to listen carefully.

"This glider is known as a Waco CG-4A. It was the type used during World War II. But, relax, guys, because this ain't an old model you'll be flying in. This one is fresh built off of old blueprints. I did the job in an empty hangar at McChord Air Force Base next to Fort Lewis, Washington. And I've been able to increase the original performance by using aluminum tubing frame rather than the old steel type they had in 'em before, and I've covered it with fiberglass instead of the old fabric. That meant I could use the molding qualities of the covering and get rid of some of the support structure the original design called for. The deck is still plywood though."

Robert Falconi interrupted him. "What's the technical and capability breakdown of this aircraft?"

"Well, it's best described as a high-wing monoplane type, and it can carry more than its own weight. It weighs in at 3,440 pounds and can carry 4,060 pounds.

There's a pilot and copilot to operate it, and the glider can haul thirteen guys in the fuselage. The wingspan is a hair over eighty-three-and-a-half feet and the length of the fuselage is forty-eight feet. The maximum towing speed should be around one hundred and twenty miles an hour. I figure the stalling speed around fifty, but we'll find out for sure about that during the flight tests."

"Hey!" Archie Dobbs exclaimed. "This thing ain't even been flown yet?"

"Nope," J.T. answered. "And that brings me to the part of my little spiel where I introduce the pilot. Orville, stand up."

Orville, looking a bit embarrassed, got to his feet.

"That little guy," J.T. continued pointing at him, "is one of the finest sailplane pilots in America today — maybe in the world. We'll find out when he gets into that class of competition. When I designed my aircraft for the 1961 championships, I chose him to pilot it because I knew he could get the most performance from my baby. And he did. When we fly into Laos, you can be sure that the guy working the controls will get every inch of lift possible out of those wings. Now, any questions?"

"Yeah." Calvin Culpepper stood up. "Just how far will this here glider . . . *glide?*"

"I estimate a glide ratio of one-to-fifteen — fifteen feet forward for every one it drops," J.T. answered. "Which means we'll be released from an altitude of ten thousand feet in order to be able to travel the approximate thirty miles to the landing zone." He knew he was stretching things a bit, but he didn't see any point in worrying the other men unnecessarily.

Falconi joined the young designer. "If you have any more questions for J.T., save 'em for later. Incidentally, he's a veteran of the Korean War—infantry commo man. He'll be operating the radio in the glider." Falconi pulled a sheet of paper from his pocket. "Now I'm going to break you down into teams and then we'll get into the actual conduct of the attack and your various roles in it. Rather than waste a lot of time reading off a roll, I'll post it on the wall here. Find out which leader you belong to; get him and we'll continue."

Falconi tacked the list on the bunker bulkhead and stepped aside to allow the Black Eagles to find out their exact assignments.

COMMAND & SCOUT ELEMENT
Capt. Robert Falconi, Commander
Sgt. Archie Dobbs, Scout
PO2c. Sparks Jackson, Radio Operator
Sfc. Malpractice McCorckel, medic

GLIDER CREW*
Sp4c. Orville Hanover, Pilot
J.T. Beamer, Copilot

DEMO TEAM
S. Sgt. Calvin Culpepper
CPO Popeye Jenkins

FIRE TEAM ALPHA
1st Lt. Dinky Dow, Team Leader

S. Sgt. Tom Newcomb
Sfc. Horny Galchaser, Grenadier
S. Sgt. Calvin Culpepper**

FIRE TEAM BRAVO
M. Sgt. Duncan Gordon, Team Leader
S. Sgt. Lightfingers O'Quinn
M. Sgt. Chun Kim, Grenadier
CPO Popeye Jenkins**

* To remain with aircraft during raid on target.
** Assignment after demolition phase of the operation.

CHAPTER EIGHT

The pilot's voice crackled over the radio speaker. "Black Eagle, this is Mother Hen. Still with us? Over."

"Roger," J. T. Beamer said into the microphone. "We'll be running some handling tests, so wait for our directions. Keep going straight and level at this altitude. Out." He turned to Orville sitting in the pilot's seat. "How's she doing, Orv?"

"I'll let you know in a little while," Orville replied getting the feel of the controls.

It hadn't taken the Black Eagles long to assemble their glider. Within a couple of hours the flying machine, painted with the same camouflage pattern as the men's tiger fatigue uniforms, had been wheeled out on the air strip. The C-123 tow ship had arrived that same morning and little time was wasted in putting together a flight test.

No passengers accompanied Orville or J. T. during this first trip upstairs. If something went wrong—and that was a distinct possibility—Captain Robert Falconi didn't want to lose any more men then he possibly had to.

Orville checked his simple instrument panel. All he had mounted there was an altimeter, compass, and three indicators which told him the rate of climb, turn and bank, and air speed. Suddenly the glider began buffeting. The skinny pilot's hands bounced and vibrated on the wheel.

"Damn it!"

"Get her outta the tow plane's slipstream, Orv!" J. T. exclaimed.

Orville pulled back on the control column and the aircraft responded clumsily but settled down once they were positioned slightly above the C-123 ahead of them. "I guess this baby won't ride in that turbulence, huh?"

"Won't seem to," J. T. agreed. "Sure ain't like a sailplane behind a Cessna-140, huh?"

"Nope." Orville made a few experimental pushes and pulls while working the rudder. "Let's try a turn to the left."

"Right," J.T. said. He spoke into the microphone. "Give us a long, slow turn to port."

"Roger," the pilot responded.

Orville looked out at the three hundred feet of nylon tow rope that connected them to the airplane that towed them through the sky. It had stretched at least fifty feet beyond its original length.

One of the things that Orville had to concentrate on during the maneuver was to make sure he didn't over-anticipate the tug pilot's actions and react too quickly. If he began his own turn too early he would be inside the tow rope. That could result in the glider being suddenly jerked forward with such an increase in speed that a climb would result — or the rope would break.

On the other hand, if Orville was too slow and ended up too far to the outside, it would be like the ice skater's game of crack the whip and would require a lot compensation on his part to get back into proper position.

But the young pilot did the job beautifully, waiting

until he had reached the tow plane's position in the sky before beginning his own smooth maneuver.

The turn took five slow minutes. But Orville was definitely not happy. When they straightened out he scowled. "This thing isn't handling right, J.T. It's sluggish as hell and I'm working my ass off."

"Okay. Let's try the trims then." He reached overhead where three crank pulleys were located. These operated the trim tabs on the ailerons, rudder, and elevators. He worked them, getting nods of approval from Orville as he adjusted the setting to relieve the pressure on the controlling surfaces of the glider.

"Hey! A hell of a lot better," Orville said.

"Right. We got to start thinking big, Orville. We got a hell of a lot more aircraft here than we're used to."

"Let's take it down," Orville said.

"Right." Again, J.T. spoke into the microphone. "Mother Bird, bring us around for a landing. Give us enough altitude for a three-sixty. Out."

The two flying machines, one towing in the other, swung slowly through the sky and lined up on the airstrip. Orville could see the landing area over the top of the C-123. "Cut loose."

J.T. reached upward and grabbed the big red knob that was located on the windscreen supports over the sparse instrument panel. He pulled and their forward speed immediately slowed so much they leaned forward. "Off tow!" he said into the microphone.

The big airplane's engines roared with added power and it turned to the left out of their way.

Orville applied gentle stick pressure to the left. The big glider banked in that direction in response to the deft action. At the same time he put on just a touch of left rudder. He held on until the amount of bank he desired was reached, then he neutralized the controls.

He maintained a bit of back pressure on the wheel to keep the nose from dropping, and was satisfied to see that the horizon rode smoothly as it appeared to swing around in front of them. He used one of the windshield braces as a reference, keeping it even with the dancing green of the ground that seemed to tilt precariously in front of them.

The terrain rolled slowly and gently until, finally, he could see the asirstrip. This indicated that they had gone in a complete circle.

Now Orville was ready to try a landing.

He pushed down on the control column in an easy movement, and the glider tilted forward and went into an extremely shallow dive. "I want to get down faster than this."

"Yeah," J.T. said. "Remember, this thing is designed to carry a load. And we have no ballast aboard."

"Looks like a job for the ol' spoilers," Orville said. He operated the lever by his seat and the rectangular-shaped air brakes on the upper side of each wing sprang up. This broke the flow of air over the aircraft and it sank at a steeper angle but without an excess increase in air speed.

"Drag chute!" Orville called out.

"Roger," J.T. responded. He pulled another handle, and once again, their forward progress was noticeably slowed.

Orville sat the glider down as though he'd been flying that same one all his life. The wheels barely bounced; then they rolled smoothly across the hard-packed run-way until the skid brake was applied. The large craft came to a stop even with the area where the Black Eagles stood waiting.

The men, despite their inexpertise in this type of flying machine, approached it to perform a meticulous inspection of its exterior as Robert Falconi trotted up to the cockpit. "What's your verdict, Orville?"

Orville, a bit nonplused because he hadn't quite gotten used to an officer calling him by his first name, cleared his throat. "It's a good ship, sir. A few more flights and we'll be ready to go."

"That's the spirit!," Falconi said. He turned to the team sergeant. "Let's turn her around and get ready for another takeoff."

"Yes, sir!" Duncan Gordon motioned to the men. "Shake it up! The tow plane is coming in, so let's move this glider around for the next flight."

After the powerless aircraft was positioned and the rope reattached to the C-123, they watched as another test began with the fiberglass ship being hauled once more into the hot tropical sky.

After it was airborne, Master Sergeant Gordon motioned to Archie. "Come with me, Dobbs."

"Sure, Sergeant," Archie responded coldly.

He followed the top NCO off the airstrip and back through the camp to their bunker.

When they arrived, Duncan motioned him inside. "Get your entrenching tool and get right back out here."

"Right," Dobbs said puzzled. He went to his gear and pulled the small shovel from its carrier on his patrol harness. He returned to the detachment sergeant. "Now what?"

Duncan led him to a spot behind the bunker. He pointed to the ground. "There! I want a hole six feet wide, six feet deep and six feet long."

Dobbs' face reddened with anger. "Are you havin' me dig a fuckin' *Six-By*, Sergeant?"

"You got it right."

"I don't believe this shit," Dobbs said.

"You'd better believe it," Gordon said in cold anger.

"This is Special Operations Group, for Chrissake!" Dobbs exclaimed. "And in a combat zone!"

"I want a Six-By, Dobbs," Gordon said. "I don't give a damn if we're on a suicide mission inside the Kremlin."

"I ain't had to do such a chickenshit thing since Basic," Dobbs protested.

"There's one thing you're going to learn mighty fast, Dobbs," Duncan said coldly. "You don't give me any shit—none at all. You told me to *cram it* at a formation I called with this whistle of mine."

Dobbs grinned insolently. "I sure as hell did."

"So now, I'm telling you to *dig it*."

An expression of defiance crossed Dobbs' face. "Maybe I ain't up to this crap."

"I can't make you dig that Six-By, Dobbs," Gordon said.

"That's right."

"But I can sure as hell make you wish you had dug it," the master sergeant retorted. "Now what's it going to be?"

Dobbs was silent for several moments. Then, wordlessly, he positioned the digging blade of the entrenching tool and slammed it into the ground for the first stroke.

"And I want those sides straight and smooth."

Dobbs, his emotions boiling with anger, began swinging in a regular rhythm. "Right, Sergeant."

CHAPTER NINE

The Black Eagles, formed in a single line, trooped through the darkness of the camp toward the airstrip.

Completely outfitted for the mission ahead, their faces were camouflaged with grease paint daubed on in black and green streaks. Their tiger fatigues, including the narrow-brimmed boonie hats, added an ominous emphasis to their appearance. Three of the men, Calvin Culpepper, Popeye Jenkins, and Horny Galchaser, each struggled along with a pair of crater charges. Calvin and Popeye carried the fuses, caps, and detonators spread around in their gear in such a manner that one wouldn't set off the other.

Other members of the B-camp garrison looked on in silence as the fourteen men passed the various bunkers. Seeing teams and detachments on their way to dangerous operations was a familiar sight to the Special Forces troopers. Many of these soldiers, sitting outside their bunkers drinking beer, had either recently returned from their own missions or were scheduled to go out on operations in the near future.

Most watched the procession in silence, but now and then one would grin in encouragement and give the old thumbs-up signal as best wishes.

When they reached the waiting glider, Master Sergeant Gordon halted them. Orville and J.T. entered the aircraft first and settled into their seats in the Plexiglas front to begin their preflight check.

Then the rest of the Black Eagles filed in. Captain Falconi, Archie Dobbs, and Fire Team Alpha took the port side. Malpractice McCorckel, Sparks Jackson, and Fire Team Bravo settled in on the starboard row of seats.

It was 2328 hours.

The final stages of the briefback, in which all members of the team recited their particular roles in the upcoming activities and answered all questions directed at them, had been concluded at noon that day. After some minor supply negotiations conducted by Lightfingers O'Quinn, the men were left alone — confined to the bunker but allowed to spend the remaining hours until departure, reading, sleeping, playing cards, or engaged in whatever activity they desired.

Orville and J.T., with an armed escort to insure no contact with outsiders, had been required to make four separate trips out to the aircarft on various business that involved both the glider and the tow plane. Last minute coordination and rechecking between all flight crews involved in the operation was essential if the flying stage of the mission were to come off as planned.

Now Orville completed the check-out routine. He looked over at J.T. in the dim red glow of the battery-powered illumination of the instrument panel. "Looks good."

"Right." J.T. turned to look at Falconi. "We're ready, Cap'n."

Falconi checked his watch. It was 2241. "Let's have a commo check with the tow plane."

"Yes, sir." J.T. picked up the microphone. "Mother Bird this is Black Eagle. Commo check. How do you

73

read me? Over."

The aircraft responded with, "I read you five-by-five, Black Eagle. Over."

"Roger. Wait."

"Tell him we'll take off on schedule," Falconi said.

"Mother Bird, we'll lift off at 2400 hours. Over," J.T. said.

"Roger, Black Eagle. Out."

It was 2343 hours.

There was silence in the narrow fuselage. Each man was wrapped tightly in his own thoughts. Most were reviewing the individual jobs they were to perform in the attack.

2345 hours.

The C-123's engines, previously warmed up, kicked over, the prop wash making the glider vibrate a bit.

The Black Eagles felt confident, knowing the element of surprise was on their side. *Maybe the thing would be a piece of cake*, they mused. *Of course, the Pathet Lao are all over the place.*

But the seven men of the detachment who had participated in the murderous Song Bo Slaughter also recalled how recent it had been that unexpected enemy troops in an operational area inflicted thirteen casualties on a force of twenty-one men. Fire Team Bravo, led by Top, had but one survivor—Lightfingers O'Quinn. And of the five guys in Fire Team Alpha, only Horny Galchaser and Calvin Culpepper had come out.

2350 hours.

The radio came to life and the pilot spoke tersely to them over the instrument. "Black Eagles, This is Mother Bird. Moving to take off position. Over."

"Roger, Mother Bird," J.T. responded. "Out."

The roar of the C-123's engines increased and so did the glider's shaking. Orville could barely make out the tow rope as it straightened out while the tow plane taxied away.

Archie Dobbs, his hands sore from digging the Six-By, licked his wet lips. His mind turned over the satisfying thought that he might pull the pin from one of his grenades and drop it down the back of Master Sergeant Gordon's fatigue jacket. Fragging the strict sergeant was such a pleasant idea, it made Archie smile to himself. He began to mentally devise other forms of torment and revenge he would like to perform on the senior NCO.

2400 hours.

"Black Eagles, this is Mother Hen. Cross wind from eleven o'clock. Ready for take off? Over."

"Roger, Mother Hen. Out."

The nose of the glider bounced a bit, then Orville could feel his craft moving behind the big tow plane. He kept his eye on the flaming exhausts of the C-123 as he pulled back on the control column. The humming of the craft's rubber tires on the airstrip ceased and they eased up while the big plane pulling them was still on the ground.

Orville gave some left rudder pressure and crabbed into the wind. The C-123 rose into the air and the young glider pilot worked his controls to stay above it.

"Jettison landing gear," Orville said.

"Roger." J.T. worked another lever and their wheels dropped off to spin downward through the tropical night. It had been thought that landing on jungle grassland spread over bumpy terrain could be done better with a skid rather than wheels that might catch in a hole or depression and flip the glider.

They had only had time for a couple of night flights, and Orville now wished they'd had two or three hundred more. He could see absolutely nothing except the exhaust and momentary glimpses of the tow plane against the clouds now that they were climbing.

"Black Eagle, this is Mother Bird. How you doing? Over."

"This is Black Eagle," J.T. answered. "Everything's fine back here. Over."

"Roger. We'll continue to altitude. Out."

The climb was horribly slow and monotonous. Although they would be going a bit higher than ten thousand feet there was no oxygen for anyone except Orville and J.T. Not only was it thought unnecessary for such a short ride, but there wasn't much of the breathing gas available. And when even the scrounger-*par-excellence* Lightfingers O'Quinn couldn't get his hands on any bottles of the stuff, it was a sure sign there was none other available in their area of operation.

The flight continued smoothly, with the drone of the C-123 now a minor irritation in their ears. Archie Dobbs' mind was now concentrating on pictures of Master Sergeant Gordon up to his neck in a violently boiling pot of chicken fat.

J.T. tapped Orville's shoulder. "Ten thousand feet," he said indicating the altimeter. "Oxygen."

The two donned the masks and Orville continued flying while his copilot turned on the valves. They were approximately two miles up now, well above the heavy tropical atamosphere of the lower altitudes. Their release point was to be determined by the air force navigator in the big airplane ahead of them. The plan was that, on his word, they would get off-tow and turn on a magnetic azimuth of three hundred and ten degrees for a free glide of approximately fourteen-and-a-half miles.

0130 hours.

Robert Falconi dozed in the dark. He wished he could see his men. It was good for morale to be able to talk to the guys and keep their spirits up with a little humor during these first — and worse — hours of an operation. Normally, in a parachute infiltration, he would walk up and down between the rows of jumpers and chat with them. Cracking jokes and exchanging wisecracks relieved the tension to a great extent.

Sitting there in the dark, with only the dull glow of the instrument panel for illumination, could become unbearable after a while. Falconi remembered when he had met an ex-RAF bomber pilot several years previously. The man had flown many bombing missions over Nazi Germany during the war, and Falconi had asked him what the worst part of those missions was. The man had replied quite candidly that the scariest part was the time when the crews were having their night vision readied for the coming operation by sitting in dark rooms that were lit with only a single red light bulb. "It gave the chaps time to turn over in their minds the awful danger they would soon face," the pilot had said, "and how bloody stupid they were for volunteering as bomber crews to begin with. Bad show."

0201 hours.

"Black Eagles, this is Mother Bird. Prepare to go off tow. Over."

J.T. reached up and grasped the knob. "This is Black Eagle. Ready. Over."

"This is Mother Bird. Wait . . ."

Fourteen throats turned dry and swallowed with

77

great difficulty.

"Wait . . . now!"

J.T. pulled. "Roger. Off tow!"

The roar of the C-123's engines quickly faded away, leaving only the sound of the wind rushing past the glider as it settled into a normal flight.

Orville made a sweeping starboard turn, maintaining it until the compass swung around to three hundred and ten degrees. On course," he told J.T.

"Right." The copilot rummaged in the canvas bag at his feet and brought out the US/F metascope. From this point on, he would be sighting through the device while Orville turned all his attention to the glider's flight instruments.

"Altitude nine thousand, nine hundred feet," Orville announced.

"Right! Off oxygen," J.T. said, pullling his mask from his face as Orville did likewise. He put the metascope to his eye and looked forward out of the cockpit.

"See anything?" Orville asked.

"Not a thing," J.T. answered.

Infrared light is made up of invisible rays just beyond red in the visible spectrum. With an effect of penetrating heat, these are shorter than radio waves. Special devices, such as the metascope, make it possible to see such infrared light. Other apparatus that produce infrared allow the user to literally see in the dark if full and properly equipped.

The Black Eagles' landing zone would be paralleled by a series of this type of light that would be invisible to the naked eyes of any passing Pathet Lao but clearly obvious to J.T. utilizing the metascope.

"Nine thousand, one hundred," Orville said. He

made a turning correction to maintain the proper magnetic heading.

"I hope those fly boys cut us off at the right angle and place." J.T. said still sighting through the device. "I don't see shit."

"You'd better get the landing zone on the radio," Orville said.

J.T. grabbed the microphone with one hand and held on to the metascope with the other. "Bird's Nest this is Black Eagle. Over."

"Black Eagle, this is Bird's Nest. Over."

"This is Black Eagle. Is the LZ lit up with the infrared? Over."

"Affirmative. Are you coming in now? Over."

"I sure as hell hope so," J.T. said. "Out."

They glided on, the wind whistling past the aircraft, as the men peered intently outside into the inky blackness.

"Five thousand," Orville said.

Falconi leaned forward. "See anything yet, J.T.?"

"Nope."

The glider yawed slightly and Orville applied rudder pressure to bring the nose back into position. Holding the right heading and keeping the descending craft in complete control was difficult.

"Two thousand!"

"Goddamn it!" J.T. swore.

Everyone was nervous now, with the exception of Archie Dobbs. In his mind, he had drifted off into a world where fierce-faced demons stuck red-hot pitchforks into the bare ass of a screaming, sobbing Master Sergeant Gordon.

"Eight hundred feet!" Orville said breathlessly.

"Damn, J.T.! You must see something now."

"Nothing!"

Falconi's voice boomed out loudly. "Crash positions!"

The men leaned forward, eyes shut tightly and teeth clenched in anticipation. Archie Dobbs snapped out of his reverie. "Hey, guys," he said cheerfully. "At least this ain't like a regular airplane. No gasoline to blow up, huh?"

"What about these fuckin' cratering charges?" Calvin Culpepper asked.

"Oh, shit!"

"Three hundred fucking feet!"

J.T. peered through the metascope, then suddenly the yellowish-white column of lights showed up. "Three degrees right."

"Two hundred feet!"

"Two degrees right!"

"One hundred feet!"

"One degree left!"

"Hang on!"

The glider bumped into the ground and the sound of grass swishing beneath them filled the fuselage as in the skid, they skimmed over the terrain. J.T. leaned on the brakes and their craft gradually slowed; then the forward motion stopped and they abruptly halted, the tail rising from the force of the stoppage.

As soon as the rear of the glider hit the ground again, Falconi leaped into action. He opened the door of the fuselage and led Alpha Team out. The Bravos followed and a hasty perimeter was set up.

Falconi moved forward toward the jungle that encircled the landing zone. A figure stepped out of the shadows and spoke in an American-accented voice.

"What's happening?"

"A bird is looking for a nest," Falconi responded.

"We have one for a black eagle."

With the proper recognition code established the two closed up enough so that they could see each other. Falconi recognized the man as an intel sergeant from the 5th Special Forces. "Howdy, Buck," he greeted him.

"How're you, Cap'n Falconi?" the sergeant replied. "Welcome to Laos."

CHAPTER TEN

The sun was only a dull red glow above the eastern tree lines. Captain Falconi, now satisfied that his men were properly placed for the attack that was due to begin in slightly less than half an hour, moved silently through the thick brush on his lone reconnaissance patrol.

Not wanting any nasty surprises, Falconi had decided he would feel better if he personally assured himself of the location of enemy troops in the area.

The glider, with Orville Hanover and J.T. Beamer guarding it, had been hauled into the tree line and quickly camouflaged. Even intense scrutiny could not have spotted the aircraft unless an intruder practically walked into it.

Their target, the site of the nuclear plant, turned out to be a wide cleared area three hundred meters across. A basement floor of cement had been laid in the deep excavation scooped out of the jungle earth. Six tall columns of steel-reinforced concrete rose majestically from that solid platform to form the basic skeleton of the structure. Notches in the large objects gave evidence that steel girders would be added to them, and the walls and floors of the facility would be contructed on and around these supports.

The center of the unfinished building was wide open, leaving space for the deadly breeder and its various cooling and auxiliary features and attachments. Falconi's blood ran cold at the thought of insane prophets and followers of the most fanatic brand of Communism known gaining the potential ability to produce atomic fuel.

The 5th Special Forces man, Sergeant Buck Martin, had given him a brief and sketchy rundown on the happenings in the area. It was an incomplete picture, mainly because Martin and his men hadn't spent much time on ops in the vicinity. The guerrilla group was made up of anti-Communist Laotian tribesmen whose homeland was located in a different area some fifty kilometers away. In fact, Falconi had been told, they'd moved in specifically to provide a landing zone for this mission. They had no base camp and the locals were definitely not overly friendly toward them. Martin's guerrilla band had looked forward to the arrival of the Black Eagles. Now all they had to do was keep a corridor of escape open between the objective and the glider for a couple of hours.

Then they could get the hell out of this hairy place.

There were numerous, very strong and reinforced units of the Pathet Lao in the operational area. The guards around this site were but a splinter detachment, but they seemed to be well organized and alert. Of all the many sentries spotted, none had been dozing. That was a sure sign of a well-trained and disciplined outfit.

Falconi moved around in some confusion. His peculiar talent for keeping himself physically oriented helped him to maintain his location in relation to the target. But, not knowing the terrain well, Falconi suddenly stumbled out of the brush and onto a well traveled trail.

The Pathet Lao soldier he literally bumped into was as surprised as the American.

For one instant they stared at each other and Falconi considered bringing up his M-16 and blowing the bastard away. But the noise would take away the surprise of their attack — and the Red was unarmed. Evidently he had been out answering nature's call and was on his way back to his billet or sleeping area.

Falconi, moving with such rapidity that his action was very close to being one of blind instinct, brought up his left leg and lashed out with a pivot kick. He fully expected to send his opponent crashing to the ground.

But the man skillfully turned away and flowed with the maneuver avoiding all contact. The Red followed this up with an explosive snap of his right arm. His hand, in a knife-edge position, slapped into Falconi's weapon, knocking it whirling into the bushes.

The American assumed the front-guard position, semicrouched, and waited for the Pathet Lao to make his next move.

It wasn't long in coming.

He threw a side kick toward Falconi's groin. When it didn't connect, the man tried a quick series of finger jabs toward the eyes and a sweeping roundhouse punch to the jaw.

Falconi ducked under the first attack and blocked the wild blow with his left forearm; then he moved with lightning speed to close with his opponent. He grasped the Red's shoulders and stepped in with his left foot just outside of the man's right ankle. At the same time, the Black Eagle executed a cross-hock takedown by throwing his right leg into the back of his opponent's left, tripping him. The man was on the way to the ground when Falconi slipped his knife free and drove it downward.

The blade slid easily into the soft spot in the sternal

angle between the breast bone and the Adam's apple. The soldier gurgled and blood poured from his lips and nose. At the same time his eyes rolled back until only the whites showed. A couple of brief shudders and then the body went limp.

Falconi wiped the knife off on a pants leg and replaced it in the scabbard strapped to his boot. Then he pulled the dead man off the trail and out of sight into the bushes. After retrieving his rifle, he headed back to the detachment.

When he arrived at the attack position, Archie Dobbs looked at him with open curiosity. "How the hell'd you work up such a sweat, Skipper?"

"Ran into an official greeter," Falconi said. He checked his watch. "0520 . . . ten minutes 'til the attack."

Major Truong Van of the North Vietnamese Army Intelligence Service hurried down the hall of the staff building toward the communications center.

Before his assignment to work directly under Lieutenant Colonel Gregori Krashchenko of the Russian KGB, Truong had liked to enjoy a leisurely cup of tea at his desk before beginning his day's work. But the Soviet officer, in his zeal, not only opened their office at five o'clock each morning, he didn't even allow any time to properly prepare for a long day's work. Truong was expected to leap into his tasks the moment he arrived. But this morning, in a fit of rebellious feeling, he had stopped long enough to get some tea in the building's canteen. Then he made his usual report to see if there were messages for them at the communications center.

The young girl in charge of the incoming message desk displayed a toothy grin and handed him a large envelope full of official letters and documents. She looked at Truong through her black-framed, thick glasses. "You must have very important work, Comrade Major. All of this had to be decoded."

If she'd been more attractive—and that bastard Krashchenko wasn't up there waiting for him—Truong might have taken the opportunity to try to strike up a meaningful relationship with her. But, instead, he was officially proper. "We have a most demanding assignment. Please see that any additional incoming papers are forwarded to us immediately. There should be more in the next delivery."

"Yes, Comrade Major," she said. She displayed an open, inviting smile.

Truong, despite her rather plain looks, let his mind toy briefly with the thought of seducing her but quickly regained his composure. "Thank you, Comrade."

He hurried back upstairs to the isolated office he shared with Krashchenko.

The Russian colonel impatiently took the envelope from him when he arrived. He scanned the messages inside. "Ah! The reports on the American officers currently on detached duty within Southeast Asia." After reading a few moments, he burst out with a wide grin. "Mmmm, we have something here."

"Is it someone in Commando X?" Truong asked.

"I don't know if he's a member of that elusive group or not, but the preliminary information here is most interesting," Krashchenko explained. "It seems that one of the officers on our list is a Soviet citizen."

"How can a Russian serve as an officer in the American army?" Truong asked.

"Very simple. By American law, he is not—and has

never been—a citizen of the Soviet Union. But by our statutes he belongs to us because his mother was Russian and illegally left our country," Krashchenko said.

"I don't understand why the great Soviet Union would even have a regulation like that," Truong remarked candidly. Then he quickly added, "what is the advantage of giving strangers such privileged status in the worker and peasant paradise?"

"The advantage, Comrade Major Truong, is that if we get our hands on him we can treat him as one of our own," Krashchenko explained. "That allows us to put him on trial as a traitor, to shoot him, imprison him, or do whatever we desire through our court system. Some of our reeducation specialists might even be able to persuade him to see things our way or get him to agree to become a propaganda tool in exchange for better treatment."

"Then, without a doubt, it would be most desirable to have that particular officer captured and brought north?" Truong asked.

"Exactly," Krashchenko answered. "I presume you'll have no trouble seeing that he is located and caught through the efforts and facilities of your own espionage and intelligence nets."

"None at all," Truong answered. He was happy that he could say something to favorably impress the Russian. "All we need is his name and any other information you have about him."

"His name," said Krashchenko, "is Falconi, Robert Mikhailovich. A captain in the 5th Special Forces. That is all I have."

Truong grinned. "That is all we need. If this Captain Falconi is anywhere is Southeast Asia, our people can find him. I will tend to this matter immediately."

"Good," the KGB colonel said. "Now let us turn our attention to Commando X."

Master Sergeant Chun Kim, the South Korean marine representative on the Black Eagles, examined the M-79 grenade launcher he carried. He opened the weapon and inserted one of the dozen 40-mm rounds he carried in his ammo pouches into the chamber. He snapped it shut and pushed the safety forward to place it on fire.

He settled down and picked out a good target. A sentry stood next to one of the concrete pillars that Calvin Culpepper and Popeye Jenkins were going to blow.

Their attack position was a semicircle. Across from them, in an area where they could avoid friendly fire, the Command and Scout Element — Falconi, Dobbs, Sparks, and Malpractice — formed a killer team to deal with any potential survivors of the attack who might attempt an escape. They covered the only way out of the place.

Nearby, Dinky Dow checked his Bulova watch and noted the second hand swinging around toward the twelve. Five seconds before it got there, he brought his rifle to his shoulder and took a sight picture on a Pathet Lao who slouched with an AK-47 slung on his shoulder.

Dinky Dow counted, "One . . . two . . .three . . . four . . ." His finger tightened on the trigger and the M-16 barked. The .556-mm round zipped across the open space and smacked into the Red's chest. The man's arms flew up and he collapsed to the ground.

Chun sparked off a round from the M-79. At the

same time, Horny Galchaser, his counterpart over in Alpha Team, also fired a grenade into the construction site.

The resulting explosions threw shrapnel and bits of concrete at the other sentries. The flying debris slapped into their bodies, leaving gaping, bloody injuries while knocking them into mangled heaps. Two of them, wounded, were in shock. They struggled back to their feet and met a hail of M-16 rounds that spun them around and dropped them back to the ground.

Calvin Culpepper and Popeye Jenkins rushed forward with their explosives. Tom Newcomb, helping out by carrying two of the crater charges, was close at their heels. One of the large explosive devices was dropped off at each of the pillars rising above the floor of the site.

The entire guard unit had been eliminated as the demolitions crew tended to their task. They worked rapidly in the sudden silence, while the fire teams turned their attention outward to await the expected assault from that direction.

There were holes five feet deep beside each of the pillars. These were for anchoring the legs of the breeder when it arrived. Calvin and Popeye carefully slid the explosives into these openings.

These explosives were packed in metal containers. Cylindrical-shaped and waterproofed, they had cap wells and detonating cord tunnels which were attached to each for the primers. There was also a booster charge on top to increase the assurance of proper detonation.

Calvin and Popeye, working with rapid professionalism and skill, began the fusing and capping process of the deadly devices.

Within fifteen minutes they were stringing the

detonating wires back to blasting machines waiting in the jungle.

Gunfire broke out in Fire Team Bravo's section.

Master Sergeant Duncan and Lightfingers swept the jungle in front of them with a magazine load of rounds on full auto. At the same time, Chun Kim sent two of the 40-mm grenades into the same trees. Their efforts were rewarded with screams and the sight of two bloodied Pathet Lao falling from the thick brush out onto the cleared ground of the plant site.

Calvin and Popeye reached the blasting machines and hooked up the wires in rapid, sure movements. Sweat glistened on the black sergeant's face as he worked. "I'm happy as hell that Sparks Jackson had enough sense not to use his radio until we set these babies off."

"No sweat," Popeye said tightening down on the last set of wires. "Sparks is a SEAL. He knows the chance of blowing them charges in our faces from transmitting radio waves."

"Just the same," Calvin said finishing his task. "I'm glad he don't owe me any money."

"Yeah," Popeye agreed. "You ready?"

"Roger that."

By then a full-scale battle was developing on Bravo's side of the site.

"Let's blow 'em." Calvin took a deep breath. *"Fire in the hole!"* He called out three times. It may have seemed he was going too much by the book, but Calvin wanted to make sure each and every member of detachment had ample warning in order to be able to avoid the half-dozen explosions.

The Black Eagles ducked. Those that were able rolled behind fallen logs or other jungle debris. Gordon,

Lightfingers, and Kim were unable to take cover, but luckily, they were a few meters past the recommended safety limits anyway.

The six blasts went simultaneously, the detonation sweeping across the area with a thunderous roar. Dust, rocks, dirt, and chunks of cement blossomed upward in the eruption. At the same time, the pillars leaned slightly, then quickly collapsed and broke open, revealing the twisting, bending steel-girder skeletons in their interior. Although it was hidden from sight in the clouds of flying dirt and debris, the floor of the potential nuclear plant had split open, and in some places the ground underneath had given way due to the miniature earthquake that Calvin Culpepper and Popeye Jenkins had caused.

Falconi yelled over at Dinky Dow. "Cover the Bravos as they pull back to this side of the perimeter." He motioned to Archie and Malpractice. "Lend some fire power there."

Sparks Jackson turned his attention to his radio in order to raise Bird Nest and let them know the Black Eagles would be coming through on their way back to the landing zone.

Chun Kim sent another grenade flying into the vegetation that served as cover for the Pathet Lao attackers; then he joined Master Sergeant Gordon and Lightfingers as the entire Bravo Team scurried to join the others under the covering fire provided by those same comrades.

They linked up with the rest of the detachment at the same time that Calvin and Popeye showed up.

"Let's discourage any potential pursuers," Falconi said. "Direct all your fire in the direction the Bravos came from."

The Black Eagles' impromptu combat line exploded sending a hail storm of steel-jacketed slugs slapping into the jungle across the now-demolished construction site.

Sparks Jackson motioned to Falconi to join him by the radio. The navy man was worried. "I can't raise Bird Nest, sir."

"Damn! They're supposed to be holding that corridor through the brush open for us," Falconi said.

"It'll be a hell of a note if that part of the operation is fucked up," Sparks said.

"Yeah," Falconi said. "But nobody said this job was going to be easy." He thought for a moment. "Raise the glider."

"Aye, aye, Skipper," Sparks said. He turned on the radio. "Black Eagle, this is Falcon. Black Eagle, this is Falcon. Over." After several minutes of trying he looked up at the detachment commander. "Can't get 'em. I don't know what the problem is."

"We'll play it by ear then." Falconi motioned to the team leaders. "Withdraw back to the LZ."

Malpractice and Archie Dobbs joined him. The latter slapped a new magazine into his M-16. "Do I have the honors, Skipper?"

"Right, Archie," Falconi said. "Lead the way." He knew that Archie's unerring sense of direction would get them back to the glider quick and sure. "But be careful. Sparks can't raise Bird's Nest or Black Eagle on the radio."

Archie pulled the charging handle on his rifle. "Right. I suppose this operation is going to start being all fucked up from this moment on, huh?"

"Jesus! I hope not," Falconi said. "We sure as hell don't

need another Song Bo Slaughter. Move out, Archie."

"On my way, Skipper!"

As the scout disappeared into the jungle ahead, Falconi turned and motioned the other Black Eagles to follow. The commander hoped he knew where he was taking them.

CHAPTER ELEVEN

The jungle had grown extremely quiet after the fire fight—too quiet. And Sergeant Archie Dobbs, leading the Black Eagle detachment back to the waiting glider, didn't like it one damned bit.

He halted for a moment to kneel down and perform one of the scout's most basic functions—silent observation. He waited and listened, letting his instincts work at their maximum potential. His senses, after countless bloody encounters with the enemy, had been honed to razor-sharp alertness.

Although Archie could discern no tangible evidence of a hostile presence, he felt uneasy.

After a few minutes, he got back to his feet and moved cautiously and silently out of the thick brush, back onto the narrow game trail that led to the landing zone. His eyes darted back and forth in an attempt to pick out something unusual or out of place in the primitive surroundings, and his ears were still tuned for the crack of a twig or the rustle of leaves to betray any potential ambusher.

The sudden swish of tree branches startled Archie so much he almost inadvertently squeezed off a round from the M-16 rifle he carried.

Fifth Special Forces man, Buck Martin, his hands tied behind his back, hung by his neck from a rope strung across an overhead tree branch. He had been swung out into the middle of the narrow path.

Martin's face was purple and twisted from the awful death he had endured, his swollen tongue forced out between his lips as his cadaver dangled at the end of the noose.

Archie grimaced instinctively. A Pathet Lao leaped out onto the path and screamed triumphantly, "Now you die too, Yankee!"

The American pumped the trigger on his weapon into the zealot's body, cauing the enemy soldier to stagger back under the impact of the .556-mm slugs. Then Archie turned and sprinted for the rear.

A splattering of AK-47 fire followed him kicking up dirt at his heels and breaking off bits of leaves and bark from trees as the Black Eagle scrambled for safety. He looked back when he heard the ominous ping of a released grenade safety spoon.

He saw the explosive device sailing lazily toward him, and Archie's adrenaline went into overtime. But the grenade hit a nearby tree and bounced away to explode harmlessly off to the side.

When Archie the rest of the detachment he found that Horny Galchaser and Tom Newcomb were waiting to cover his retreat. He dove past them and they immediately sprayed lead in the direction of his pursuers.

Falconi hurried over to his scout. "What happened up there, Archie?"

"Damn . . . Skipper!" Archie panted. "An ambush . . . the bastards must've . . . got Martin and his guys . . . during our attack. They'd strung . . . the poor bastard up . . . and swung him out at me on the trail. I damn near . . . had a fuckin' heart attack!"

"We're going to have to take a detour to get back to the glider," Falconi said.

"If there's a glider to get back to," Archie remarked.

"That's all we need," Falconi said. He looked over at Sparks Jackson. "Have you been able to raise the glider yet?"

"Negative, Skipper," Sparks answered. "Want me to try again?"

Yells and wild bursts of gunfire broke out immediately ahead.

"You'd better wait, Sparks," Falconi said. "We gotta get the hell outta here."

The Black Eagles broke contact by setting up a leap-frog withdrawal in which the teams alternately covered each other's rearward movement. First the Alphas laid down a base of fire while the Bravos traveled a short distance back. A determined line of Pathet Lao rushed them, but the ill-advised assault was swept away and the Communists were blown into bloody chunks by the curtain of .556-mm slugs blasted at them.

Then, with the Bravos keeping other enemy attackers at bay, the Alphas ran past them and stopped to turn and fire. This gave the Bravos the opportunity to get out of harm's way.

It was a good maneuver, but the benefits were only temporary.

When they were finally able to put a respectable amount of distance between themselves and the Pathet Lao, they formed a hasty defense perimeter. Sparks Jackson, sitting in the middle with his radio, turned his attention to the microphone he held in his sweating hand. "Black Eagle, this is Falcon. Over."

All he heard was the hissing from the receiver. "Black

Eagle, this is Falcon. Over." After several more tries he gave up.

"Can't get 'em, Skipper," he said.

"They were probably wiped out with Buck Martin and his bunch," Falconi mused.

Archie Dobbs was confused. "How come they got our guys while we were attackin' the plant site? You'd think the Gooks would have come after us first."

"It was because that Pathet Lao unit ran into them on the way to the assault. The bastards couldn't just ignore 'em and come after us. They had to deal with them first," Falconi said. "It was Martin's tough luck the LZ ended up between us and an enemy outfit."

Malpractice McCorckel, who had been on a two-fold mission of fetching the team leaders as well as checking out any wounded, reported in with Dinky Dow and Master Sergeant Gordon. "No casualties, Skipper," Malpractice said. "We're all healthy."

"Except for the LZ party and our glider crew," Falconi said. He motioned to Dinky Dow and Gordon. "Sit down, we've got to figure out a couple of things here. The situation is all fucked up at this point. We may or may not have our escape aircraft available, and, even if we do, our landing zone security has been wiped out. We're going to have to figure a few new courses of action here."

"The first one is plain enough, sir," Gordon said. "The outfit we just broke contact with is going to be closing in with us within a quarter to half an hour. Our primary job will be to fight them off."

Falconi nodded. "Yeah. Looks like we're in for one hell of a battle in as matter of minutes."

Major Andrea Thuy tapped on Chuck Fagin's door and stepped in. "We've just gotten the word that the Black Eagles were inserted on schedule."

Fagin got up from his desk and walked over to the large map of Southeast Asia mounted on his wall. He studied it for several long moments as the young Eurasian woman joined him.

"That's where they are," he said laying his finger on the exact spot where a red pin had been stuck. "Amidst all those topographic symbols denoting ridge lines, swamps, rivers, and jungle, our boys are doing their job."

"Let's hope it goes better than the Song Bo fiasco," Andrea said.

"I'm not real familiar with that one," Fagin admitted. "Clayton Andrews ran the operation. I understand there was a matter of misinformation, right?"

"Not exactly *mis*information," Andrea said. "It was a bit out of date. An area thought to be occupied only by a part-time village militia and a second-rate prison guard detachment turned out to have a full-strength NVA infantry battalion right in the middle of it."

"I see," Fagin said. "Well, this time we knew beforehand that there were strong, numerous enemy units in the area. It's a tough situation, but as long as things go smoothly there should be no problems."

"I should have been with them," Andrea remarked bitterly. "Then and now,"

Fagin sighed. "We've been over that before."

"When the CIA sent me to Langley for intensive training and instruction in English, they did not mean for me to sit at that desk out there!" she exclaimed angrily.

"And the didn't mean for you to fall in love with Captain Robert Falconi either," Fagin retorted.

"I have personally assassinated three NVA officers, two Communist bigwigs in Laos and Cambodia — not to mention eliminating a Russian propaganda official in a Hanoi alley," Andrea said coldly. "I also participated in Operation Hanoi Hellground. And my contribution and professionalism was noted there too."

Fagin was adamantly impersonal and cold. "Your efficiency and usefulness decreased rapidly the first time you went to bed with Falconi. There is absolutely no way in hell that any case officer is going to put you two out in a combat situation together. Any play of strain on emotions could cost you not only your own lives but could also result in the deaths of others and a mission blown wide open."

"But, Chuck —"

"And you know it!"

Andrea's face reddened. She agreed that losing control of her emotions and falling deeply in love with Robert Falconi was a professional error. But the feminine side of her personality had finally triumphed over the soldier's side for the first time in her life. The bitter hatred in her heart and the desire to fight her enemies had been overwhelmed by the tender feelings she'd developed for the handsome American.

Fagin continued. " Now we can't send you out into the cold for fear of affecting Falconi. What do you think will happen to his concentration if he knows you are out on a mission? Your situation would be in the back of his mind to the extent that he could very well make some mistake — perhaps not a stupid, glaring one but enough of an error to prove costly and excessively damaging to our operations."

The Oriental part of Andrea's ancestry caused her to lower her eyes in acceptance of this chastisement. "Yes . . . yes, I understand."

Fagin controlled his temper which had been approaching the boiling point. When he'd first learned of Andrea Thuy from Clayton Andrews, he'd been excited at the prospect of having such a valuable agent on his staff. His disappointment and anger had been indescribable when he'd finally figured that she and Falconi were hopping into bed together.

That was the worst possible thing that could happen between two agents or operatives.

Fagin walked back to his desk. "Keep me posted on any incoming scoop on the operation."

Andrea nodded. "Yes, Chuck." She walked silently out of his office to her own desk in the other room.

Chuck Fagin waited until she shut the door; then he turned his attention back to the map. The indicated locations of Pathet Lao units were shown in red grease pencil on the acetate covering of the topographical chart. The CIA man licked his dry lips as he noted the thin corridor that offered the only escape route from the target area to the landing zone.

A slight delay or missed communication could mean the complete wipe-out of the mission — not to mention the Black Eagles themselves.

Master Sergeant Gordon knelt behind the tree waiting for the first sign of the approaching enemy. He glanced to his right at Chun Kim. The Korean marine looked back and waved, the M-79 grenade launcher he carried loaded and ready for action.

Beyound him and out of Gordon's sight, Lightfingers O'Quinn lay in a natural depression in the jungle ground, his M-16 pointed toward the potential attack.

Gordon glanced to the left and saw the UDT demo expert, Popeye Jenkins, his own rifle ready, peering intently into his fire zone.

The detachment's senior NCO knew that all these were good men, and he appreciated their fieldcraft and combat efffectiveness. What he disliked so intently was their haphazard approach to discipline and military protocol. Gordon, after years of service in some of the army's elite ariborne units — the 187th Airborne Regimental Combat Team. the 11th Airborne Division, and the 82nd Airborne Division — had developed an asspreciation of orderliness and regulation. He didn't like the way the men addressed their commander by his nickname, nor their sloppy appearance, nor the way they conducted themselves in the camp where they stowed their gear away in any haphazard fashion around their bunks. Each man kept his pack, canteens, pistol belt, and other field gear in his own individual manner giving the sleeping quarters a sloppy appearance.

The Black Eagles slept on GI air mattresses, using poncho liners as covers. While it would have been impossible to have made-up bunks under those conditions, Gordon had tried to get the Black Eagles to roll the liners up and put them back in their packs during the day. But they always seemed to forget.

The master sergeant had already made up his mind to break Archie Dobbs a couple of ranks when they got back too. *Shipping the insubordinate bastard off to a stockade wouldn't be a bad idea either,* Gordon told himself. *But, on the other hand, Dobbs is one hell of a good tracker and —*

The attack broke out with a roar of automatic weaponry fire that swept their position.

Gordon's Fire Team Bravo bore the brunt of the Pathet Lao's preliminary effort. They poured fire back at the short, attacking figures of the enemy soldiers who charged forward in compact, screaming groups. The first waves collapsed under the Black Eagles' bullets.

Kim's grenade launcher barked and it's small missile streaked out to explode among the guerillas. The deadly bits of shrapnel blew down the Reds who had been unlucky enough to get caught within the ten-yard killing radius of the ammunition.

The Pathet Lao continued to press their attack, the dead piling up while the living fanatics leaped across the cadavers to be caught in the Bravos' intense fire that Gordon directed so effectively.

But the carpet of enemy dead slowly drew closer to them until the senior noncommissioned officer realized the pressure had neared the breaking point. The small-fire team now faced being overwhelmed and drowned by the pressing numbers of the fanatical attackers.

"Fall back!" Gordon shouted. He turned toward the rear and hollered again, this time to Dinky Dow and the Fire Team Alpha. "Cover us! We're pulling in!"

Lightfingers and Popeye, on the flanks, scurried back while turning now and then to spit lead at the pursuing Reds. Kim fired his grenade launcher one more time and then turned to join the withdrawal.

Archie Dobbs had gone forward with the Alphas to lend his fire power to their's during the onslaught. He watched as Lightfingers and Popeye, running like hell, crossed the perimeter and then turned to meet the onslaught that trailed them.

A couple of beats later, Gordon appeared. He dove behind the log barriers that Dinky Dow and his men had hastily rolled into position. The master sergeant wasted no time in checking out his team.

"O'Quinn!"

"Here, Sergeant," the marine answered.

"Jenkins!"

"Yo!"

Chun!" Gordon looked around. "Where the hell is Chun?"

"He ain't showed up," Archie said. The scout spotted a couple targets and pumped out three quick rounds, sending the Pathet Lao stumbling into the soft jungle earth.

"Christ!" Gordon said. He leaped to his feet and charged over the logs.

"Hey, Sergeant!" Archie yelled at him. "You can't go out there!"

Dinky Dow grinned. "He go anyhow. Look for Kim, huh? Crazy idea to run at Pathet Lao."

Archie nodded. "Yeah. Well, if he catches one we won't have no more bunk inspections back in camp."

But within moments, Gordon appeared lumbering toward them, the small stocky Korean across his back. A howling Red bearing a machete chased after him. Archie stood up, took careful aim, and dropped the zealot with one shot.

Gordon hopped over the logs and fell, spilling Chun Kim to the ground. The Korean's forehead was cut and blood flowed down his face.

"Medic!" Gordon called out.

Malpractice appeared and went straight to the injured man. He gave him a quick examination; then he set to work bandaging him up. "Not serious," he explained to Gordon. "Looks like he must've stumbled and bumped his head."

Archie took a look at Master Sergeant Gordon. *Chickenshit sonofabitch's got balls*, he said to himself. Then he turned his attention back to attack that once again pressed heavily down on them.

CHAPTER TWELVE

Colonel Ngai Quang of the South Vietnamese Army Special Intelligence Group finished shaving his sparse whiskers and wiped the soap from his face.

He was a short, extremely thin man in his middle years. Despite the smallness of his frame, a slight paunch was beginning to develop and it protruded slighly over his belt. The graying of his hair was kept under control with an over-the-counter remedy he purchased at the various American PXs he visited on a regular basis.

The colonel was in a bad temper. The mah-jongg game the night before had turned out to be an unmitigated disaster. He was out almost a hundred thousand piasters.

Ngai could hear his wife speaking to someone over the hum of the air conditioning. He pulled on his tailored gabardine uniform shirt and stepped out of the bathroom into his house's spacious master bedroom. "Who were you speaking to?" he asked testily.

"The maid," his wife answered. "She brought in the dry cleaning. It just came over from Tan Son Nhut." The couple preferred the superior quality of the cleaners on the air base to the sometimes careless and shoddy civilian operations in downtown Saigon.

"Are any of my uniforms there?"

"I'll see," Mrs. Ngai said. She opened the large bag that had been draped over the clothing. "Yes . . . a couple."

"Good," Ngai said. "I'll check them over."

"Why are you so critical? You know they do a good job over there."

"I must be very careful of my appearance," Ngai snapped at her. "I deal with high-ranking officials of not only our own army but that of the Americans."

He was not particularly fond of his wife. His marriage to the squat, homely daughter of a business associate of his father had been arranged. Ngai, knowing that his family disapproved of his choice of the military as a career, agreed to the nuptials to ease his parent's unhappiness.

He went to the clothing laid over the bed and pulled out his uniforms, carrying them over to his own closet. "Is breakfast ready?"

"Probably not," Mrs. Ngai replied.

"Go see," Ngai said curtly.

"The maid will call us when —"

"I said *go see if breakfast is ready!*"

When she left the room, Ngai tiptoed to the door and peered through it to make sure she'd gone. Then he softly shut and latched it before hurrying back to the uniforms. One was hung on a hanger that was slightly different than the others. Ngai took it from the closet and pulled the uniform off. Next he carefully removed the cardboard tubing from the wire. He slipped his fingernail into the small slit along the bottom and pried it open. A tightly rolled sheet of paper fell out. Ngai picked it up and quickly shoved it in his pocket. Then he replaced the uniform and returned it to the closet.

A minute later he joined his wife for a breakfast of fresh fruit and daintily fried fish. Colonel Ngai was in a much better mood.

The fighting had driven the Black Eagles over three kilometers west of their landing area.

Their situation was not enviable. They were far from friendly territory, and trapped in an area that literally crawled with Communist guerrillas and soldiers. The civilian population, even if they did hate their Red masters, were so terrified of the authorities that the infiltrators could never count on them for aid of any kind.

The original exfiltration method in the mission's plans was in serious doubt for several reasons. The main problem was that they didn't know if the glider they used to land in the operational area was in enemy hands or not. And, even if it wasn't, the chance of setting up a retrieval by having a tow aircraft come in to pick them up seemed to be growing more remote with each passing hour.

At least the Black Eagles were healthy.

The only casualty so far had been Sergeant Chun Kim. But his injury was only slight. He'd stumbled and fallen to the ground during the withdrawal, striking his head on thick, exposed root of a tree. But he had been only momentarily unconscious, recovering soon after Master Sergeant Gordon had carried him to safety.

Now, after again escaping from a pressing enemy unit, they enjoyed the temporary and fragile safety offered by a tangled clearing in the jungle trees.

Captain Falconi motioned to his radio operator, navy SEAL Petty Officer Sparks Jackson. "Try to raise the glider again."

"Yes, sir." Sparks turned to his An/PRC-41 radio. "Black Eagle, this is Falcon. Over." He waited a moment and then spoke again. "Black Eagle, this is Falcon. Over."

After several minutes of trying, Falconi shook his head at the commo man. "Forget it."

"Aye, aye, Skipper," Sparks drawled. "I reckon the Pathet Lao got their asses, huh?"

"I don't know, but I would imagine so," Falconi said.

"That's a real shame," Sparks said. "That little ol' Orville Hanover was good feller. Kinda liked him. And J.T. was okay too."

"Yeah," Robert Falconi agreed solemnly. He disliked discussing missing or dead comrades. Despite his best efforts, Falconi always felt an attachment to the men under his command. His two team leaders, Lieutenant Dinky Dow and Master Sergeant Gordon, sat with him. The captain sank into deep thought for a while, chewing on a blade of grass while he turned over the situation's alternatives in his mind. "Anybody got any ideas?"

"Sure," Dinky Dow popped up. The diminutive little ARVN officer never seemed to be discouraged. "We go south to base camp. Kick ass all the way, huh?"

Falconi grinned despite the gravity of the situation. "We just might do that, Dinky Dow." He glanced at the detachment sergeant. "What do you think, Gordon?"

Gordon frowned at the omission of his rank, but he stuck to the subject. "We weren't given any particular contingencies, sir. I suggest we make a try for the exfiltration as per the operations order."

"And what if the glider isn't there?"

Gordon shrugged. "Then we 'E and E' back to friendly lines."

"Escape and Evasion no fun," Dinky Dow said. "I say again—kick ass!"

Gordon looked at the Vietnamese. "I don't think there's a lot of chance of our kicking ass from this point on. We'd be better off thinking of *saving ass*—our own."

"Well put," Falconi said. "By the way, that was a hell of a thing you did in pulling Kim away from the Pathet Lao."

"It was my job," Gordon said coldly. "I was the closest and the rest of the men had already reached safety."

"I'm putting you in for a decoration when we get back," Falconi said. "There was a tactical advantage involved. You saved a support weapon."

"It was only an M-79," Gordon said. "And with three rounds left, it won't be giving us support much longer."

"You're getting a medal whether you want the god-damned thing or not," Falconi said, a bit angry. "Sounds like you don't care much for decorations."

"I already have a couple," Gordon said.

"You're a real cold fish, aren't you?" Falconi asked.

"I'm a professional soldier, sir," the sergeant replied.

"So am I, Gordon."

"I most respectfully request that you use my rank when you speak to me, Captain," Gordon said.

"That's your right . . . *Sergeant,*" Falconi responded.

Archie Dobbs, sitting close by, leaned over to Malpractice and whispered in his ear. "Can you believe that shit? He's gotta be the most RA motherfucker I've ever known. And I figgered that chickenshit bastard would be crazy for ribbons to pin on his chest."

"He'll be getting a star on his Combat Infantryman's Badge," the medic said. "Maybe that's enough for him."

Falconi, on the other side of the clearing from them,

109

stood up. "Whatever we do, we can't stay in one place very long. This place is teaming with Pathet Lao."

"What course of action have you chosen, sir?" Gordon asked.

"I'm taking your advice, Sergeant Gordon," Falconi said. "We'll make a try to return to the glider. But that's our second priority."

"What's the first, sir?"

"Staying alive."

The sentry presented arms at the doorway and Colonel Ngai returned the salute as he hurried into the building of the Army of the Republic of South Vietnam's intelligence branch.

This edifice, its color brilliant white in the hot sunshine, was surrounded by a thick wall of masonry. Located in Saigon not far from the presidential palace, a half-dozen separate strands of barbed wire fence had been erected beyond the structure, and there were guard towers situated at each corner of the compound. Each of these posts boasted a .50 caliber Browning machine gun along with rocket launchers. The latter weapons were to be used in the event of a vehicular attack. Roving guards on foot and in jeeps enhanced this tight security.

Colonel Ngai was well known in this section of the military staff, and the troops detailed there were well acquainted with him. They required no identification from Ngai as he proceeded into the building's interior where his own office was located.

Ngai had a staff of a dozen people who worked under him in his particular job. Their function was to maintain the files of information he supervised. These were devoted to individuals, friendly and enemy, who figured in the clandestine activities of the evergrowing conflict in South Vietnam.

Although their work did not involve actually going into the field, their nitpicking and cross-checking had resulted in the discovery not only of enemy agents actively engaged in spying and sabotage, but in the arrest of several extremely clever double agents.

Ngai stopped at the sergeant major's desk to pick up his mail and messages; then he went to his adjutant to check out the furlough list that had just been drawn up. After a few curt exchanges with other members of his staff, Ngai retreated to his office.

He shut the door and locked it.

Colonel Ngai Quang had spent almost twenty years in the military. First in the colonial army under the French and then in the Army of the Republic of Vietnam when that was established. He had been an exemplary officer in the performance of his duties.

It was an off-duty vice that proved his undoing.

Gambling, if it can be an obsession for the Occidental, is even worse for the Oriental who succumbs to the temptation to earn big money through the roll of the dice, turn of the card, or — as in Ngai's case — the draw of the mah-jongg tile.

The officer gambled long, hard, and desperately in the gaming parlors in the Chinese quarter of Saigon. The angry, wild, and illogical bets Ngai made soon caught the attention of agents and operatives who had been placed and financed in such businesses by their Communist employers.

Their primary duties were to spot people known to be in sensitive government and military positions who dis-

111

played marked weaknesses at the gaming tables.

Once they were able to determine his identity, Ngai received special attention from them and from their shills who participated in the games.

At first he began to win huge amounts of money. He could do nothing wrong in his playing, and his luck was never bad as night after night he left his favorite mah-jongg parlor with his pockets crammed full of piasters. Then Colonel Ngai's luck slid a little, picked up, slid back a bit more, rallied slightly, and then he again won big—for the last time.

After that his luck plunged to the depths and he soon amassed a sizeable debt to Tsing Chai, the owner of the parlor he frequented. Ngai was so obsessed with gambling that he was unaware all his fortunes—and misfortunes—had been skillfully manipulated by the wily Chinese.

Within a year and a half, the situation was impossible. He faced both professional and personal ruin and found himself at Tsing Chai's mercy.

Tsing Chai was an extremely corpulent individual who wore expensive silken robes and kimonos over his expansive girth. He was well known in various vice and criminal circles of South Vietnam's capital city. But even the police had no inkling of his espionage connections with the north.

The Chinese gambling chief approached Ngai in a sympathetic, friendly manner about the great amount of debt the army officer had amassed in his establishment.

"Ah, my dear Dai Ta Ngai," Tsing Chai said to him. "You're luck has been most wretched lately. I am so sorry."

"As am I," Ngai replied sadly. "I fear I have reached the limit of your kind advance of credit to me. I owe you much money."

"Let us go into my office and discuss this most unhappy situation," Tsing Chai said. He led the army officer to his office located in the back of the parlor. They had settled down with tea and rice cakes. After a few minutes of enjoying the refreshments, Tsing Chai spoke again. "There is a way in which you could ease your debt to a considerable extent."

"I would be most anxious," Ngai said hopefully.

"And, I might add, you would also find yourself in receipt of even more credit." Tsing Chai displayed his most magnanimous smile.

"I am most grateful," Ngai said. Even at that point he had secret misgivings, but his compulsion to gamble overshadowed even these intuitive feelings that were reinforced through a thorough schooling in intelligence.

"I require a list of names, that is all," Tsing Chai said. "If you could get it for me, I would consider your bill fully paid and forgotten."

Desperately, Ngai agreed and ended up supplying the Chinese with a relatively harmless roster of the recent graduates of the ARVN's intelligence school.

The gambling went on, and so did the demands. Before he was fully aware of how far the situation had gone, Ngai found himself turning over top secret documents. And, although he received huge sums of money for them, he gambled the cash away in more rigged mah-jongg games. Ngai became so compromised, that, at any time, Tsing Chai and his cohorts could have turned over the evidence they had on him and the Vietnamese officer would have been summarily court-martialed and shot.

Ngai had fallen into the classical trap. In his case there was no way out except death — no alternative, no contingency, only death, either by firing squad or suicide.

He decided to get what he could out of life until that last awful moment, and he became an agent, taking the money and practically handing it right back through his uncontrollable devotion to gaming.

In order to keep his spirits up somewhat, Tsing Chai saw to it that certain extras and luxuries — such as an air-conditioned house — were provided that would keep Ngai thinking of what his illegal acts had gained him. At least he couldn't gamble the house, maid service, and the expensive clothes for his wife away without attracting some very unhealthy attention. The Chinese vice entrepeneur also saw to it that many of Ngai's bills were paid, thus easing his financial status to a great degree while allowing him to continue playing mah-jongg.

This act was not all out of generosity. If Ngai had been allowed to accrue many debts, he would eventually gain the attention of South Vietnamese counterintelligence. Then his entire life — and Tsing Chai's espionage and spying operation — would be uncovered.

Now Colonel Ngai Quang sat in his private office. The door, as usual during highly classified activities, was locked from the inside, so he had no reason to fear an unexpected intrusion by one of his staff.

He slowly rolled open the paper that had been concealed in the hanger from the Tan Son Nhut air base cleaners. It was in code, and he lifted the false bottom of the desk drawer to get at the slender, compact decoding book kept there.

It took him fifteen minutes to decipher the message.

First he had to get the proper key word and write it down. After that he drew a diagram under it which consisted of numerous squares. Then he laboriously printed the letters of the message in the squares.

Another similar diagram was made with the letters in the key word now transposed into alphabetical order. The message from the original was rewritten in the new order until, finally, his instructions were spelled out clear and concise:

MOST IMPORTANT. REPLY IMMEDIATELY. FIND EXACT UNIT LOCATION OF FOLLOWING AMERICAN OFFICER RECENTLY DETACHED FROM 5TH SPECIAL FORCES GROUP: CAPTAIN ROBERT MIKHAILOVICH FALCONI

CHAPTER THIRTEEN

Master Sergeant Duncan Gordon, his M-16 locked and loaded, stood behind the tree and stared out into the jungle ahead of him.

He had gotten a permanent reinforcement for his fire team in the personage of Sergeant Dobbs. Falconi had decided to remove his scout and medic from the Command and Scout Element and put them out with the riflemen to beef up their combat effectiveness. He assigned Malpractice McCorckel to Dinky Dow's Alphas but kept Sparks Jackson and his radio with him during this hectic period.

It seemed they were being chased from one end of the jungle to the other by the numerous units of Communist Pathet Lao that had converged on the scene of the nuclear power plant's destruction.

Gordon heard faint rustlings ahead of him. He brought up his rifle and waited. The first Red soldier appeared a scant ten yards ahead of him. The sergeant aimed carefully; then he squeezed the trigger. The man chosen as a target bounced back from the slug that slammed into his chest. He collided into a tree behind him and spun around in time to catch the second shot in the back of the skull. The bullet exited through his right eye carrying with it brains, blood, and flesh that splattered the nearby plants.

A round zapped past Gordon's left ear and he turned in that direction. A Pathet Lao aimed the Kalashnikov AK-47 for another attempt, but the American was faster. Two bullets from the M-16 punched into the enemy's bony carcass and threw him like a pile of rags into the thick undergrowth.

Tree bark exploded by the master sergeant's head. Gordon returned fire again but the enemy trooper who had shot at him ducked. Shots came from another direction, then a third position as the air around the master sergeant buzzed with whining bullets.

Gordon flipped the selector switch to full automatic and cut loose with short bursts of fire at the places he figured the shooting was coming from. But the incoming rounds increased, and he found himself pinned down.

It would only be a matter of minutes before they closed in.

Gordon prepared for his final moments by ejecting the now-empty magazine and inserting a fresh one.

But suddenly a rally of fresh shots came from the rear. The bullets flew over his head into the enemy lines. They were followed by the appearance of Archie Dobbs and Lightfingers O'Quinn who now covered him.

"Move back, Sergeant Gordon!" Lightfingers yelled. He fired a fusillade to the right while Archie did the same on the left.

Gordon, not wasting one valuable second, turned and sprinted toward them. When he drew abreast of the two Black Eagles, he turned and added his own fire power to theirs as the trio moved back.

Finally they were back with Alpha Fire Team. Gordon wiped the stinging sweat from his eyes and glanced at Archie and Lightfingers. "Thanks."

"Sure, Sergeant, don't mention it," Archie said. Then he and the marine went back to their positions on the line.

A minute later an explosive eruption of shooting and screaming broke out on Dinky Dow's right flank. Tom Newcomb and Horny Galchaser were occupying that part of the line.

Pathet Lao, with no regard for their personal safety, ran at the two. The Australian fired rapidly at any target of opportunity that appeared in his sights. The momentum of their running caused the Reds who were hit to continue to stumble forward a few steps before finally hitting the ground in undignified bundles of dead humanity.

Horny fired the last two rounds of the grenade launcher, the small explosions tossing the ripped-open bodies of Pathet Lao into the air. Then the Cherokee Indian unslung the M-16 from across his back and joined Tom Newcomb in setting up a steel curtain for the Red guerrillas to run into. The enemy did exactly that, piling up between the trees in growing numbers.

Over on the left flank where Master Sergeant Gordon's Fire Team Bravo had pulled in to form a tighter defensive position, the Pathet Lao tried a flank attack.

Chun Kim, now with only one round left for his M-79, pulled back and turned to face this new contingent of fanatical assault troops. He fired the final grenade in such a way that it would explode off a tree some six feet above the ground. The resulting detonation sent the shrapnel flying in a miniature air burst that mowed down a half dozen of the attackers.

Gordon, Lightfingers, and Archie Dobbs took up the

slack with their rifles, their uncoordinated but deadly volleys, sweeping the Communist fighters off their feet in rows.

This assault, only a probe by the Red commander, broke off and the pressure on that part of the perimeter eased.

But the center of the Black Eagles' position, where Calvin Culpepper and Dinky Dow were located, found the brunt of the enemy effort concentrated on them. They desperately pumped bullets into the closing enemy, spilling dozens of the Asians to the ground. Falconi and Sparks joined them to beef up the fire zone. The pressure tapered off; then a sudden quiet engulfed the scene.

"They've pulled back," Calvin said.

"Yeah," Falconi said. "But only to regroup. This is a do-or-die effort on their part. They'll either wipe us out, or we'll do it to them."

"If anybody's taking a vote, I vote for us," Calvin said. He held up his M-16. "And this is the best fuckin' ballot around, baby."

"It sure as hell is with the M-79s gone," the Falcon said. He decided to take advantage of the lull. "Sparks, try to raise the glider again."

"Aye, aye, Skipper." Sparks Jackson set his radio down and tilted the whip antenna in the direction of the — hopefully — waiting aircraft. "Black Eagle, this is Falcon. Over." He rechecked the frequency setting. "Black Eagle," Sparks repeated. "This is Falcon. Over."

After five minutes had passed Falconi nodded toward the navy radioman. "That's enough. Save the batteries."

"I'll bet them damn Pathet Lao hung ol' Orville and J.T. like they did that sergeant from the Fifth," Calvin said.

"Probably," the Falcon agreed.

"We in same fix like Song Bo, hey, Falcon?" Dinky Dow asked.

"Well . . . yes and no," the Falcon said. "First I'll give you the good news in relation to that. We've got effective commo gear now. We might be able to set up a chopper exfiltration. But that's only a maybe—a very weak maybe. But in this situation that's the best we got."

"So what's the bad news, Falcon?" Calvin asked.

"We're a hell of lot farther away," Falconi said. "That'd put a real bad strain on a helicopter unit reaching us. And remember what happened to our last planned chopper extraction."

"Yeah," Calvin said sullenly. He recalled seeing the aircraft sent to pick them up shot down by North Vietnamese Mig-17s only a short distance from the landing zone.

"Want me to do like I did on Mau Xanh River, Falcon?" Dinky Dow asked.

"Wouldn't do us much good in a case like this," Falconi replied. "Cutting a few throats in that mob out there won't help us a bit."

Archie Dobbs scurried in from the outer perimeter. "There's movement all over the place, Skipper," he said to Falconi. "Looks like they're encircling us."

"Okay, thanks, Archie," the Falcon said. "We have no choice but to tighten up. Tell Gordon—*Sergeant* Gordon, that is—to bring you Bravos in and hold the east half of our defensive circle."

Dinky Dow got to his feet. "I go tell Horny and Tom to pull in." He trotted off into the brush in front of their position.

The Black Eagles defense was organized within the limits of a small elevation of ground. Although there was only scant advantage in being able to look downward at attackers through thick jungle, it at least gave them somewhat of an edge. And the closeness of the vegetation, while giving Falconi's men good cover and protection, broke up the mass attacks the Pathet Lao seemed to favor.

But, as Captain Falconi knew all too well, any advantage they enjoyed was destined to be overcome by the numerous, pressing ranks of the Communist zealots. And there was no sure way for the Black Eagles to get the hell out of there.

Their defeat was only a matter of time.

The closeness of their perimeter made it possible for Falconi to address all his men. "You grenadiers bury those M-79s. We have no ammo for them anymore, and there's no sense in letting them fall into enemy hands. Break the launchers into pieces. Put the stock assemblies and receiver groups into one hole, then the barrel groups, sight assemblies and fore-end assemblies into another. Got it?"

"Yo!" Horny Galchaser called out.

"Yes, Falcon," Chun Kim said acknowledging the instructions. He still had a bandage over his cut forehead.

"And one more thing," Falcon said. "Everybody fix bayonets."

There was a series of metallic clicks as the last order was obeyed. Then the Black Eagles settled down to wait.

The afternoon dragged on, the heat settling into the trees like a steaming, creeping invisible tide. Insects buzzed and birds sang while numerous monkeys chattered high above in the tall trees.

The noise ceased almost all at once.

Such absolute silence is unnatural in the jungle. The myriad of animals and insects that inhabit the densely forested and humid areas only become quiet when they sense danger or intruders in their domain.

For a full two minutes not a sound disturbed the hot stillness as the Black Eagles, their faces streaked with sweat and their lips tightly pursed together in dreaded anticipation, tried to catch sight of something—anything—through the brush that stretched out and slightly down from their perimeter.

The attack burst forth when figures of Pathet Lao, who had painstakingly crawled dozens of meters through the rain forest, suddenly leaped up and charged, their high-pitched screaming eerie in the tight confinement of the jungle vegetation.

Falcon's men, with the former grenadiers now acting as automatic riflemen in their fire teams, cut loose with sweeping volleys that sent swarms of bullets slashing into the yelling Pathet Lao.

These fanatical storm troops threw up their arms, spinning and staggering under the impact of oncoming slugs. But behind them, their wild comrades continued to push forward until they, too, had holes blown into their slight bodies before they crumpled into crimson heaps.

The enemy commander had made no attempt at subtlety or tactics. He had simply ordered the mass of his troops to get as close as they could to their objective by slithering through the stinking jungle undergrowth on their bellies and then to rush the badly outnumbered Americans.

Horny Galchaser, his M-16 on full automatic, sent

short bursts of flying bullets to back up the staccato pattern of shots that Dinky Dow, Tom Newcomb, Malpractice McCorckel, and Calvin Culpepper poured into the relentlessly pressing enemy.

Bloody carcasses were piling up rapidly in the enemy position into which Master Sergeant Gordon and his Bravos fired their overheated weapons to repel the human waves that threw themselves into the the Black Eagles' sheets of bullets.

A shrieking Pathet Lao, who had somehow made his way through the Black Eagles fusillade, leaped over the pile of his dead and dying comrades and charged the perimeter. He made straight for Archie Dobbs who, face turned slightly away, fired at the Reds pushing relentlessly toward him. Archie caught sight of the attacker a split second too late. But Gordon stepped in and ducked under two wild shots from the man's Russian assault rifle to swing a vertical butt stroke that drove the stock of his M-16 up into the guerrilla's jaw. The Red's head snapped back; then Gordon slashed down with his bayonet opening the Pathet Lao from right shoulder to the left side of his waist. Bleeding in sheets, the man hit the ground and rolled over to die.

"Thanks, Sergeant," Archie said. "That's one I owe you."

Gordon made a snap shot that dropped another attacker who had pressed too close. That man had no sooner rolled to the ground than one of his comrades leaped across him and collided with the master sergeant whose weapon had suddenly jammed. Both combatants went to the dirt, rolling and kicking. The Pathet Lao, who was smaller and more nimble, gained the upper position. He brought the muzzle of his AK-47 down to shoot directly into Gordon's snarling face.

A shot nearby exploded and the Red's nose flew off his face in a bloody spray. Another bullet hit the side of his neck and blew out the opposite jaw. Gordon kicked the cadaver away and looked to see Archie Dobbs turning to point his M-16 back to the main area of the attack.

"I always pay what I owe, Sergeant," Archie said. Then he turned back to the job at hand.

Master Sergeant Gordon got back to his feet and pumped the charging handle of his rifle. The stubborn round that had jammed was seated in time to be fired as two more enemy soldiers leaped into their position. Both died screaming their insane rage.

"Bravo Team, move back!" Gordon shouted. The Pathet Lao, in their human wave tactics, had all but overwhelmed them. He stumbled rearward to cover his men.

Archie, Lightfingers, and Popeye moved back with Chun Kim still squirting bullets at the relentless attackers whose dead now lay six feet deep in front of the defensive position.

The Bravos continued withdrawing until they backed into Dinky Dow's Alpha Team. Falconi was now in the center of the group, the fanatical Communist fighters herding the Americans together by sheer weight. The battle had, by then, deteriorated into close-in brawling in which the Black Eagles fired point blank into the attackers who were practically nose to nose with them.

Blood sprayed from bullet wounds and bayonet stabs as enemy dead, unable to fall, were pushed into the detachment's position to tangle their feet. Calvin Culpepper went down like a tackled running back when a cadaver crashed into his knees. His weapon, which he was reloading, fell across him and the magazine of bullets bounced out of his reach. Pinned down, he looked up to see a crazy Pathet Lao, his eyes wide with blood lust, raise a machete to strike. The attacker's throat suddenly turned into pulverized flesh and the man died. Calvin turned to see that Gordon had saved him with a quick shot.

The noise of the fighting stopped.

For one incredulous minute, none of the Black Eagles said a word. Then Archie Dobbs, never able to keep his mouth shut for long, spoke in the unexpected vacuum of silence. "What the fuck happened?"

Falconi wiped at the sweat that streamed down his face from beneath the boonie hat. "God damn! We killed 'em all."

Now the Black Eagles could hear moaning from wounded Pathet Lao as they looked around. Calvin Culpepper swallowed hard. "You mean ever' damn one of 'em?"

"Looks like it," Falconi said. "Archie, you and Horny run a quick recon in the area." He waited until the two had climbed the mound of dead and gone into the jungle. "Lightfingers you're the supply man. Take Tom, Calvin, and Popeye. The four of you pick out good AK-47s and load up on plenty of ammo. We're going to have to rearm ourselves." He watched as the quartet set to work. "The bastards won't have much on them, but check for any other goodies anyway. You might find something we can use. We're just about out of everything. The rest of you form a perimeter until we get ready to get the hell out of here."

Archie Dobbs and Horny Galchaser returned after a quarter of an hour of scouting the area. "You was right,

Skipper," Archie told Falconi. "We killed 'em all."

"Yeah. But only this bunch here. There's dozens more Pathet Lao units out there that'll be coming our way," the Falcon said.

"Hey, Falcon," Dinky Dow, ever enthusiastic, said. "How many more attacks like this 'til we all dead?"

"One or two, why?"

Dinky Dow grinned. "I just want to know how much Pathet Lao ass I kick before I die."

"Jesus!" Master Sergeant Gordon exclaimed at the little Vietnamese's remarks.

Calvin smiled slightly. "Now you know why we call him Dinky Dow," he said to the detachment sergeant. "That means 'Crazy' in Vietnamese."

"I see," Gordon said. "And I believe."

"By the way, Sergeant, thanks for shooting that machete totin' bastard off my ass," Calvin said sincerely. "I owe you."

"Okay," the master sergeant replied. "I think I owe a coupla guys around here too."

CHAPTER FOURTEEN

Chuck Fagin heard the tapping on his door in his subconscious. He answered it without breaking his concentration on the reports he was perusing. "Yes?"

Major Andrea Thuy stepped into his office and closed the door. "We have a message regarding the Black Eagles," she said softly.

Fagin's mind whisked away from the paperwork and he looked up into the woman's beautiful face. "Great! What's the word?"

"The USAF liaison officer reports that there has been no request for extraction from them," Andrea said stonily.

"You mean they haven't been exfiltrated from the operational area *yet?*"

"No."

"Damn!" Fagin lapsed into silence for several moments before he spoke again. "Maintain a close contact with SOG's air ops and keep me informed of the situation."

"Of course." Andrea walked to the door.

"Just a minute," Fagin said. He motioned to the chair at the side of his desk. "Sit down, Andrea."

She wordlessly obeyed, looking over at him, her face masking the turmoil inside her.

"You know; I know; and — for God's sake — Robert

Falconi knows that these missions verge on the suicidal," Fagin said. "We operate on a hair trigger of tension in this bureau. It doesn't take much to set things off. One little missed rendezvous or a slip of the tongue or even the slightest misunderstanding of orders or instructions and an operation is blown wide open. People will die."

"Yes," Andrea agreed in a whisper.

"Maybe their glider crashed in Pathet Lao territory, or they were hit at the target by an overwhelming enemy force," Fagin said unmercifully. "Ten thousand god-damned things could have gone wrong."

A tightening of the jaw was all that betrayed Andrea's mental strain. "Of course."

"If he's not out of there by now, he's probably not coming, Andrea."

"I know," she said.

"The Black Eagles could be dead or captured . . . and there's not a damned thing that can be done about it," Fagin continued.

"Are you trying to make some point?" she asked.

"Yeah . . . Robert Falconi is out there in that operational area because that is where he *wants* to be."

Andrea stood up. "Is that all?"

"You've been through a hell of a lot in your life," Fagin went on. "I just want to make sure you handle this situation in the right manner." Then he added, "I don't like displays of wild emotion."

"I won't be getting hysterical on you, Chuck," Andrea said. "Being unhappy or terribly angry is not that unusual a situation for me. But I don't think that's really what's worrying you, is it? You're looking at this from a cold-blooded professional standpoint."

"Pardon my being selfish about this, Andrea, but it

will make you a better agent," Fagin said. "If Falconi has been eliminated, just remember that you'll be under close observation. If you demonstrate you can control yourself, we'll be able to put you back on operational status."

"I'd like to be committed now," Andrea said.

"Hell, no! You're in no emotional shape for a mission," Fagin said. "You'd better inform the USAF liaison team to be prepared to scratch any planned flights involving the Black Eagles."

"I most certainly will not!" Andrea's dark eyes snapped with anger.

Fagin looked into her face, then he displayed a half-smile. "Good! I know you're not completely out of it if you still have some hope."

Andrea turned and went back to her office. She picked up the phone and told the military operator to put her in touch with the air operations officer attached to SOG.

The receiver buzzed, then clicked and a terse voice spoke. "Air Ops, Colonel Baldwin speaking."

"Colonel, this Major Thuy at SOG. You are to keep the aircraft committed to the Black Eagle operation on alert until further notice."

"Yes, of course, " the voice came back. "I just heard they haven't requested pick-up yet. Am I to presume that something's wrong?"

"Not necessarily," Andrea said. "At this point it is probably no more than a delay."

"Don't worry. And, by the way, I have a special interest in this mission. Those guys pulled me out of a hell-hole not long ago."

"You are the air force colonel that was held in Garrison Three?" Andrea asked.

"The same, lady."

"Colonel, listen to me. There is a real possibility that the mission will be aborted," Andrea admitted.

"Bullshit. Not if I'm in air ops. I'll fly in there and get those crazy bastards out myself," Baldwin said.

"Colonel, I'll keep in touch," Andrea said. "And thank you. Thank you very much." She hung up the phone feeling better. Yet, deep in her heart, she knew there really wasn't much the air force officer could do.

Her troubled thoughts were interrupted by a sudden loud knocking on her door and an MP guard shoved it open. "You have a visitor, ma'am," he announced crisply. He stepped back. "Go in, sir."

The ARVN officer, smiling and nodding to her, stepped into the office. "Ah! Good afternoon, Major Thuy."

Andrea looked up at him. "What can I do for you, Colonel Ngai?"

The Black Eagles were now completely rearmed with Russian AK-47 assault rifles taken from the dead Pathet Lao. Despite the foreign origin of the weapons, the well-trained detachment was as much at home with them as with the American M-16 rifles they normally carried. A good part of their training had been devoted to foreign military firearms, and they could not only fire them accurately but also understood the inner workings and methods of maintenance and repair necessary to keep the AK-47s in good working order.

By 1964 variations of these weapons, also known as Kalashnikovs, had been manufactured in the Communist-bloc nations for almost twenty years, making them the most widely used in the world. Any soldier from the free world who devoted part of his weapons training to that assault rifle would be very much at home in the case of having to use his enemy's equipment.

Captain Robert Falconi's men were well armed, with plenty of ammunition inadvertently supplied by the fanatic troops who had died screaming in the deadly rain of bullets sprayed out from the detachment's positions. The Pathet Lao commander, like all fanatics and radicals, let his deep belief in what he considered the righteousness of his political and ideological philosophy get in the way of logic and sound tactics. He fully expected his men to bury the raiders by the sheer weight of their numbers.

He fucked up—and died with them.

Now, two kilometers away from the scene of the last fight, the Black Eagles settled in for the night. There was no way to form carefully conceived plans. They had but one thing they could rely on—luck.

Falconi, able to relax after the fire teams had been situated in good defensive positions, sat down beside Sparks Jackson.

The navy petty officer looked over at the detachment commander. "Want me to go through the routine again?"

"What routine?" Falconi asked.

"To contact the glider, Skipper."

"No . . . wait." He thought for a moment. They really should save the batteries for contacting rescue aircraft when—and if—they got closer to friendly lines. On the other hand, it would be stupid to ignore this avenue of escape while even the slenderest thread of hope existed for it. "Let's make this the final time, Sparks. Give it a try."

Sparks turned the set on and checked the frequency setting. He picked up the mike and pressed the transmission button. "Black Eagle, this is Falcon. Over."

Only the hissing of dead air sounded over the receiver.

"Black Eagle, this is Falcon. Over."

Nothing.

"Black Eagle, this is Falcon. Over."

"Falcon, this is Black Eagle. Over." J.T. Beamer's voice broke into the void.

"Hot damn, I got 'em!" Sparks exclaimed. He spoke into the microphone without regard to proper radio voice procedure. "Where the fuck have you been?" he demanded.

"This is Black Eagle, " J.T. said. "We been up to our asses in Pathet Lao. They were so close we couldn't even turn on the radio or they'd hear it. But most of 'em have pulled out and gone now. The others in this area are a ways out from our location. How are y'all? Over."

"Still healthy," Sparks said. "But them little bastards that just left you are prob'ly out lookin' for us. Wait." He turned to Falconi. "Any messages, sir?"

"Give me the mike," Falconi said. He took it and spoke tersely. "This is Falcon. We'll be getting back to you for exfiltration. Try to monitor our transmissions as much as possible. Only turn your set off if absolutely necessary. Understand? Over."

"Roger," J.T. replied. "But the activity around here makes it impossible to use the radio whenever we want. The Pathet Lao are—oh, shit! Out!"

Again dead air sounded over the AN/PRC-41.

Falconi handed the mike back to Sparks. "I guess he had to quieten down."

"Yeah," Sparks said excitedly. "But we know the glider's there waitin' for us."

"But for how long?" Falconi asked. "And what're our chances of sneaking through a few thousand Pathet Lao to reach it? And even if we do, how can we set up for a retrieval and expect the air force to be able to send a C-123 skimming the ground through enemy fire to pick us up?"

Sparks Jackson adjusted the carrying straps of the AN/PRC-41 radio. "Looks like our situation is just a-buzzin' with all sorts o' suspenseful questions, Skipper."

"I just hope we're going to like the answers we'll be getting to them," Falconi mused.

Archie Dobbs, sitting nearby, grinned. "That reminds me o' your favorite sayin', Skipper."

"What's that?" the Falcon asked.

"Nobody ever said this job was gonna be easy!"

Chuck Fagin stood up and stuck out his hand after Andrea had introduced him. "I'm very pleased to meet you, Colonel Ngai."

"Likewise, Mister Fagin," Ngai said. He took an offered seat. "I must apologize because this first visit is not social. I have been meaning to make a call on you since I heard Clayton Andrews was transferred."

"I am most pleased to finally make your acquaintance, Colonel," Fagin said. "I understand that you worked closely with Clay Andrews on several occasions."

"Yes. And he was a good friend," Ngai said. "But I fear I am here in an official capacity rather than a friendly one at this time."

Andrea and Fagin, who both knew the function of Ngai's office, were curious. The CIA case officer asked,

133

"And what might I do for you?"

"I have this request . . ." Ngai pulled an official ARVN classified message form from his pocket and handed it to the American. "Our higher echelon requests the location of this officer."

"Captain Robert M. Falconi?"

"Yes, Mister Fagin," Ngai answered. "We learned he was a member of the Fifth Special Forces but has been detached and assigned to Special Operations Group."

"Pardon me, Colonel Ngai," Fagin said. "But this will have to be confirmed." He handed the document to Andrea who immediately left the office to tend to the procedure.

"Of course," Ngai said politely. "I would expect nothing less." He was not worried about the paper. During a routine security inspection of the message center at ARVN General Headquarters, he had deftly slipped the phony request in with other forms while going through them. It had then been properly processed and passed down to his office. Even if it were discovered to be a forgery, it could not possibly be traced to him.

Andrea returned moments later. "It's been confirmed by ARVN G2," she said. "It is listed in their communications logs."

"We don't like to give out information on our personnel," Fagin said. There was something about the situation he didn't like, but he couldn't quite put his finger on it. "Our work, of course, is highly sensitive."

Ngai continued to smile. "I understand, Mister Fagin. But the South Vietnamese army has specifically asked for this information. I don't know why someone wants it, all I know is that the man's location has been requested. I can only presume that one of our high-ranking officers needs to be acquainted with this captain's assignment." His smile broadened. "This is *our* country, Mister Fagin. And a strong agreement of mutual cooperation between various agencies is in force."

"Forgive me, Colonel Ngai," Fagin said. "I would much prefer to be given more details behind this."

"There is nothing I can add," Ngai said. "As per Standard Operating Procedure, that request for information came down to me for further action." He pointed to the paper that Andrea held. "Do you refuse to provide me with this captain's whereabouts?"

"Well . . ."

Ngai stood up. "Thank you for your time. I shall inform my superiors of the situation."

Fagin's mind raced. The one thing everyone in the upper echelons emphasized was cooperation with the South Vietnamese authorities. Even from as far back as Washington, specific orders and instructions pertaining to this had been forthcoming in a flood of directives and memos. He sighed and looked at Andrea.

"Please bring us Captain Falconi's file."

Ngai sank back into the chair. "Thank you so much, Mister Fagin. I do hope you don't hold this against me personally."

"I understand," Fagin said coldly.

Andrea returned with the cardboard jacketed dossier. She handed it to the ARVN officer. "The file cannot leave our office."

"Of course," Ngai said opening it. "I believe I will be able to get the needed information from just a quick perusal." He looked down at the papers inside. "Ah, yes, Falconi, Robert Mikhailovich . . ."

CHAPTER FIFTEEN

Lieutenant Colonel Winston Baldwin's temper exploded like the afterburner of a jet fighter.

The air force officer slammed the phone back on the cradle and leaped to his feet. He rushed into the office of his boss at the far end of the large room. The other men at their desks looked up in alarm at his furious countenance. Baldwin barged through the door without knocking and slammed it shut.

"Who the fuck aborted that mission?" Baldwin roared.

"Jesus Christ, Winston! Calm down." Colonel Robert Donaldson, his boss in the special air operations branch of SOG, was not used to emotional outbreaks. Donaldson's manner of conducting business and war was on a colder, more impersonal level. "Now what the hell are you upset about?"

"I'm pissed off about that Black Eagles mission being aborted, that's what," Baldwin said.

Donaldson thought for a moment. "Oh, yeah. That's the bunch with the glider, right? Well, they haven't called in for exfiltration and we can't hold that C-123 any longer. It's needed on some vital resupply runs."

"You know who the Black Eagles are?" Winston asked. Before Donaldson could answer, he continued. "They're the magnificent bastards that got me out of that prison camp up north. Captain Falconi and his men saved a lot of pilots plenty of future misery by eliminating both the commandant of that hellhole and the slimy little North Korean shit who was advising him on interrogation and torture of American pilots."

"Now, Winston —"

"You know who I'm talking about, don't you? The NVA colonel named Nguyen Chi Roi, right?"

"I read the G-2 report on his examination," Donaldson said.

"Aren't you kind of glad the son of a bitch has been taken out of action?" Baldwin asked.

"I'm *damned* glad," Donaldson replied.

"And we also have Doctor Yoon Hwan of the Peoples' Glorious fucking Republic of North Korea," Baldwin went on. "Are you familiar with him?"

"Of course. A principal tormentor of American pilots during the Korean conflict. He was helping to set up the North Vietnamese to do the same thing," Donaldson said.

"Yeah. But his mission was never completed, because Falconi and his men captured the miserable little bastard and killed him. That means his potential of mistreating our guys has ended. That should be worth something to the United States Air Force."

"Damn it, Winston, I appreciate that as much as you do," Donaldson snapped. "And you'll be interested to know that SOG itself instigated the abortion."

"Just because they request something doesn't mean the air force has to comply," Baldwin said. "And that includes calling things off. Hell, we've said no before."

"Not this time."

"I might add that *I* personally endured quite a bit of

137

mistreatment before the Black Eagles showed up and liberated me," Baldwin said. "And I don't see how in hell any USAF officer can issue orders abandoning Falconi and his guys when there's even the smallest scrap of hope for them."

"We have other commitments," Donaldson said. "Hell, I don't want to see those people's asses fry, Winston. But we can be stretched just so far."

"Goddamn it, Bob," Baldwin pleaded. "Keep that C-123 on alert."

"Sorry."

"They can't walk out of there," Baldwin said. "There's no way in hell Falconi's bunch could possibly get that far south without getting zapped or policed up. Their only chance is that glider."

"That C-123 has other things to do," Donaldson said.

"You've got to hold that airplane for as long as you can," Baldwin pleaded. "Two days—a day or twelve hours . . . fifteen goddamned minutes—but keep it on standby status for the Black Eagles."

Donaldson groaned. "You might as well know, Winston. You're too damned late. That C-123's been gone for four hours now. There are no aircraft to get them out."

"Then get another one. There's a mess of American airplanes in Southeast Asia, isn't there? It seems I catch sight of rows and rows of the damned things every time I go out to Tan Son Nhut."

Donaldson, ignoring the sarcasm, reached in his desk and pulled an operational roster out. He slid it over to Baldwin. "Find an available transport if you can. And take your pick. C-119s, C-123s, C-130s . . . you name it, it's committed."

Baldwin angrily scanned the paper. He handed it back. "Hell of a note."

"I'm sorry, Winston. I truly am."

Baldwin sighed angrily. "Yeah, Bob. Well, so am I. And I'm terribly sad and ashamed."

Orville Hanover and J. T. Beamer lay flat under the tail of the glider.

Twenty meters away, through the thick curtain of jungle, they could hear a Pathet Lao unit on the move. The clank of equipment and the singsong voices of their officers and NCOs added to the rustling sounds of vegetation being swept away as the unit made its way out of the area.

"Damn!" Orville whispered. "There must be thousands of 'em, huh, J.T.?"

"Yeah. That nuclear plant seemed to have been located right in the middle of one of their busiest areas."

"Think they'll find us?"

J.T. shook his head. "I don't know. It's only a matter of time. Eventually, one of them monkeys is going to stumble into here and that'll be our asses."

"When will Captain Falconi and the others be back?" Orville asked. "We were supposed to have been outta here a couple of days ago."

"Right. But you know the army, huh?"

"Christ!" Orville exclaimed under his breath. "I figgered the army might fuck up on things back in the States, but not out here in real war."

J. T. smiled sardonically. "I never thought there'd be a worse alternative to my cell in the state pen, but I'm not so sure now."

"Can you turn on the radio yet?" Orville asked.

139

"Wait'll that bunch walks on through," J.T. said.

The two glider men had endured a long period of unending tension since the landing. After the glider had been moved into an area prepared by the Special Forces sergeant and his guerrillas, a blind of vegetation had been thrown up in front of it. That had made the aircraft invisible — nearly — but now the curtain of brush was beginning to turn color as the leaves and plants it consisted of died off. A pale yellow color was developing that would be readily visible after a day or two more. Once that condition had worsened, the darker glider with its black and green stripes would be clear to even casual observers. J. T. wished they had included some yellow to the camouflaged pattern when it was painted on the fuselage and wings.

When the Black Eagles had left the glider to pull their raid on the plant site, Orville had remained in his seat. It had been thought that within a couple of hours the detachment would return and throw up the retrieval gear, and the tow plane would reappear, dive down, and yank them back up into the sky for the homeward journey.

They had waited breathlessly; then the attack on the site could be heard through the early morning air. J.T. and Orville first became alarmed at the sound of a large unit of Pathet Lao suddenly appearing from what had to be a camp quite close by.

Then firing erupted close by and J.T. rightly figured that the enemy unit had run into Staff Sergeant Buck Martin and his men. That particular fight was over long before the Black Eagles' action had quieted down.

Only fifteen minutes of calm had elapsed before more shooting flared up. This time it was closer, but it didn't

140

last long before it faded away.

"What's goin' on?" Orville had nervously asked.

"I hate to say it, but I think our guys are bein' pushed away from here," J.T. replied.

"What about that Sergeant Martin and them men of his?" Orville asked. "They're supposed to be back here to give us security on the LZ, aren't they?"

"I don't think they're coming back, Orville," J.T. said, an expression of dread on his face.

"Call in the tow plane," Orville urged him.

"I can't, goddamn it! The two of us can't erect that damned pickup antenna and push this glider out into position," J.T. argued. "Besides, from the noise around here, there's still plenty of them Pathet Lao that's been left behind."

"Like us!" Orville wailed.

The situation had deteriorated from that point on. And the pair left the questionable sanctity of the glider to hide in the nearby bush.

A Communist guerrilla unit moved into a clearing adjacent to the artificial one where the glider sat. Only a sparse ten meters of tall jungle growth separated the fanatical Pathet Lao troops from the two frightened glider crewmen who cringed in their hiding place. J.T. had to carefully crawl back into the glider and turn off the radio. The instrument, utilizing a speaker rather than earphones, hissed horribly as it waited for incoming transmissions. Eventually, despite the masking sounds of insects and animal life, one of the enemy soldiers would have heard it.

A few hours later the Pathet Lao unit moved out. J.T. and Orville smiled in relief at each other and waited anxiously for the appearance of Falconi and his men.

But, instead of the happy reunion they anticipated, they heard the distant firing of a terrific battle even farther away.

"I think the guys are being pushed out from here." J.T. surmised.

"J.T.," Orville said earnestly. "If you can't think of anything good to say, keep your yap shut. Okay?"

"I don't think I'll be talking much," J.T. remarked.

Another unit moved into the same area only lately abandoned. It became evident that the glider was inadvertently stashed beside a temporary base camp of sorts, and due to the activities in the area, it was going to be occupied quite extensively.

J.T. didn't bother to mention this to his nervous companion.

When the sound of the fighting died down once again, the two allowed their hopes to blossom anew. But nothing occurred and their hours of waiting stretched on into darkness.

The next day brought more battle noise — even farther away now — and its increased intensity had both the glider men thoroughly alarmed.

But at least the nearby camp was empty again. J.T. took advantage of the situation to crawl into the aircraft and turn on the radio. Orville stayed outside in sight, ready to signal in case unfriendly activity resumed close by.

After several hours, the hissing on the radio stopped and J.T. found himself talking first to Sparks Jackson, then to Falconi. J.T. had no sooner settled into conversation than Orville had frantically waved at him to pass the word that another Pathet Lao outfit had moved into the neighborhood. J.T. had reluctantly — but quickly —

broken off the transmission.

Now the two, still huddled behind the deteriorating camouflage, waited for the chance to get back into communication with the Black Eagles, hoping that time wouldn't turn against them.

And Orville, during the horrible moments of uncertainty, uttered the expression that was becoming his byword:

"Shit!"

Colonel Ngai Quang walked from the taxi to the door of Tsing Chai's mah-jongg parlor. He was dressed in an expensive, hand-tailored civilian suit.

The two husky bodyguards at the entrance nodded politely to him and opened the establishment's heavy ornate portal to allow him to enter.

The room was crowded, noisy and smoky. The excited conversation of the gamblers intermingled with the clatter of the mah-jongg tiles. The tables were so numerous in the room that Ngai had to turn sideways to pass between them on his way to the back of the place. The gamblers concentrated on the play with such intensity that they gave no heed to the army colonel when he bumped into them.

Ngai stopped before a huge Chinese who stood in front of a curtained opening in the back wall. The massive attendant, obviously a thug, made no indication he knew Ngai other than to loudly snap his fingers.

The draperies opened at the sound and another Oriental gangster glanced out. He looked at Ngai and, with a nod of his head, silently invited him to enter. He was taken down a short hallway and admitted through a door.

Tsing Chai, owner of the parlor, stood up behind his desk and bowed politely. "Ah! *Chao ong,* Dai Ta Ngai."

"Good evening," Ngai said returning the greeting. "*Ong manh gioi cho*?"

"I am fine, thank you," Tsing said. His wide, moon face was creased in a smile. "Please sit down and make yourself comfortable."

"*Cam on ong,*" Ngai said. He wasted no time. "I have the information you seek." He pulled his necktie up and un-pinned the paper hidden in the false fold. The sheet was filled with Ngai's own careful handwriting. It listed the facts he had memorized from Captain Robert Falconi's dossier.

Tsing Chai took the document and spread it out. "Ah! This concerns the American officer." He began to read the page of information. "So! Dai Uy Robert M. Falconi is attached to a highly secret unit under the command of SOG. . . ." He looked up delighted. "Our old friend the CIA is involved here too"—he continued the examination of the paper—". . .and is participating in highly classified missions behind the lines . . . yes!"

"That is the information you desired?" Ngai asked.

"Yes, Dai Ta Ngai," Tsing Chai answered. "Have you garnered this intelligence without arousing suspicion?"

"Of course," Ngai said. "I utilized proper channels by inserting the proper paperwork in with other documents. There is no way I can be exposed as the originator."

"*Mung ong*! You have surpassed the requirements, Dai Ta Ngai."

"*Cam on ong,*" Ngai said gratefully.

Tsing Chai reached into the wide sleeves of his Chinese robe and pulled out several small sheets of paper.

"These are your debts," he said. He methodically tore up each in its turn and dropped the pieces into a wastebasket beside the desk. "I think that should clear up the unpleasant matter."

"*Duoc roi*," Ngai said happily.

"And, naturally, once again your credit is unlimited," Tsing Chai said cordially. "Will you be playing tonight?"

"Of course," Ngai said.

"Please feel free to begin," the Chinese said. "I shall visit with you later. But first I must see that this valuable intelligence you have provided is transmitted immediately."

CHAPTER SIXTEEN

The final azimuth was plotted on the map and the line drawn from the proper contour line the shot had been taken on.

Captain Falconi, with his two fire-team leaders and Archie Dobbs looking over his shoulder, put his finger where it intersected with the previous sighting. "Here we are," he said. He moved the digit to another point on the map. "And there's the glider."

"Not far," Archie Dobbs remarked. He had been pulled from Master Sergeant Gordon's Fire Team Bravo and put back on scout duties.

"Distance isn't the factor we're worried about," the Falcon said. "It's the state of the terrain. We'll be lucky to make two or three klicks a day through the jungle. Being driven this far from the retrieval site may end up being a disaster simply because of the fucked-up geography. And there's also a large number of enemy troops located between here and that aircraft."

"Since we don't know how many there are, we'll just have to find out," Archie said calmly.

"Yeah. And it's going to be hairy. We only have one choice of action, Archie. We try to sneak through 'em," Falconi said. "We have to avoid combat if humanly possible. Keep that in mind. When we run into a Pathet Lao outfit, we do our best to squeeze by them. Or we

146

squat down and let 'em walk away without seeing us. Only if we can't avoid contact do we fight."

"More fun to fight!" Dinky Dow exclaimed. "Kick ass!"

Master Sergeant Duncan Gordon wasn't as enthusiastic. "We can fight one, maybe two more battles. After that, if we're lucky, there'll be a couple of men who might have survived and avoided capture. They'll be the only ones to make it out of here."

"Unless we reach that glider," Falconi reminded him.

"We still have to get that damned contraption in the air," Gordon said.

"Then we'll die trying, that's for sure," the Falcon said. "You want to work out any contingency plans now?"

"We don't have time, sir," Gordon answered.

"Then let's think positive from this moment on. Now here's the order of march. Archie and Malpractice take the point. Dinky Dow's guys follow while Sparks and I stay between the two teams. The Bravos will bring up the rear." He glanced at Gordon. "Make sure your last man looks behind him pretty often. Our whole ass-end security will depend on your guys."

"Yes, sir," Gordon said.

"The Pathet Lao might try that old Japanese trick the Nips used in World War II. They'd fall on the rear of a column to knock off one man at a time."

"Impress that bit of military history on the guy bringing up the rear, huh?" Falconi said. "In case of ambush I'll holler out which side of the attack we take on. Then the whole damned detachment charges that direction. We'll rally fifteen meters past the hit site."

"You don't think it'll be better to run through the ambush, sir?" Gordon asked.

"They'll have killer teams up front and, possibly, anti-personnel mines on the opposite side of their fire teams, Sergeant," the Falcon answered. "And as soon as we've penetrated their position, they'll close in the rear too. I'll make a decision when it's time to hit the flanks, and I'll do it fast. That's the exact moment we counter attack. Questions? Good, get your guys ready and briefed on the procedure. We'll move out in ten minutes."

Archie Dobbs tended to his personal gear during the short time remaining. Due to silent movement being all important, he made sure each and every loose item of his equipment was tied or taped down to avoid any rattling or the chance of being caught in the thick shrub. He had thrown away the sling on the Kalashnikov AK-47. As point man, he didn't expect much opportunity to carry it over his shoulder. The loaded rifle weighed a smidgen over ten-and-a-half pounds, quite a bit heavier than the M-16, but Archie figured he could handle that much weight without tiring to any great extent.

"Move 'em out, Archie!"

He responded to the Falcon's order by stepping into the jungle on the predetermined compass reading. Malpractice followed but a few steps behind.

The going that afternoon was slow, rough, and uncomfortable as hell. Besides the penetrating heat that drained the men's strength with its insidious humidity, the uneven terrain and clinging plant life made each step seem a separate difficult task to be performed consciously and with only the greatest of effort.

And there was the potential proximity of the Pathet Lao to contend with, too.

As more time passed, Archie had to fight the desire to give in to his fatigue and push ahead with his head down. Instead he had to stay mentally alert, his eyes darting back and forth while he tuned his ears to any unnatural sounds that didn't fit into normal jungle noises.

And there were the insects too.

A man couldn't slap at one of the biting little bastards even if it were stinging the hell out of him. The noise would have carried many yards despite the crushing density of the rain forest. He had to slowly move his hand up to the critter and mash it against his own flesh. It was messy and distasteful — but safer.

Another thing that slowed their progress was the practice of stopping now and then. This was an absolute necessity. No matter how quietly the detachment tried to move, they were bound to make noise. Periods of stillness not only confused any potentially unfriendly listeners in the area, but also gave the Black Eagles a chance to pick up sounds that might betray a nearby Pathet Lao patrol.

A few hours after starting out, Archie came across a game trail in the brush. He signaled back to Malpractice to join him. When the medic arrived, Archie whispered into his ear.

"I'm gonna check this path out. Go back to the skipper and let him know what I'm doin'."

"Right," Malpractice said. "If this trail checks out it could save us a hell of a lot of time." He went back to find Falconi.

With the Russian assault rifle held at the ready, Archie moved cautiously up the narrow track. He stayed off to the side as much as possible to give him a head start if he were forced to dive for cover. While he was concerned with any Reds that might be stationed as snipers up in trees or down in fighting holes dug within the cover of the thick vegetation, Archie was also occupied with checking the ground for signs of humans. Even the footprint of a noncombatant native would have been cause for him to abandon any idea of using the path. But Archie noted that there was not as much as an animal track in the soft earth.

He traveled two hundred meters along the trail, then put in a period of watchful waiting before he was satisfied the area was deserted.

Archie, ever careful, practiced the same precautions on his return to the team that he had used when leaving them to check out the trail. It was almost a half hour before he returned to find Malpractice McCorckel on the lookout for him.

"How do things stack up, Arch?"

"Good. We'll take the boys up that way to the place where I stopped. Then we can get 'em off into the bushes while we scout out farther ahead." He looked over at the Australian, Tom Newcomb, who was first man in Fire Team Alpha's column. "Pass the word, Tom. Let's move out."

In ten minutes the entire Black Eagle detachment was strung out along the trail. Each man had an area of responsibility to cover and secure. They kept their eyes and weapons turned in those particular directions. The men moved easier now. Although the open area offered no shade and permitted the baking heat of the sun to envelop them, it was much better than being pulled at and scratched by branches and vines in the underbrush.

The ambush blasted out from the right of the trail.

"*Right flank!*" Falconi yelled.

The entire group charged into the jungle in the direction Falconi had ordered. The Kalashnikovs rapidly chugged out their bullets in short, murderous fire bursts at the rate of 600 rounds a minute.

The Pathet Lao, not expecting the assault against them, had been in positions which offered better concealment than protection. Their plan depended on the potential victims fleeing the trail to the opposite side where land mines, designed to be activated by trip wires, had been carefully laid out.

Falconi had slung his rifle behind his back and pulled his Colt .45 pistol. He rushed through the brush and leaped into the enemy's firing position. Three very young and excited partisans looked up at the big man who had suddenly appeared in their midst. Falconi swung up the .45 pistol with both hands and pumped a round into the nearest Pathet Lao. The kid was blown into one of his buddies and both went down.

Hot air whipped by the Falcon's cheek as the third Red fired in panic without aiming. The second bullet out of the American officer's weapon smacked the guerrilla in the middle of the chest and the man somersaulted backward as if kicked by an invisible giant.

The third Red, lying stunned under his buddy, groaned. That was his biggest — and last — mistake. Falconi leaned over and performed the *coup de grâce* by placing the pistol's muzzle to the small man's ear. When the weapon fired, dust flew up from underneath the partisan's head as the bullet slapped through his skull into the ground.

At that same time, Duncan Gordon had shot one guerrilla point-blank in the face, causing the man's features to cave inward from the impact of the closely spaced two bullets.

Popeye Jenkins, just off to his left, pumped several rounds into a pair of Pathet Lao who danced into each other under the slamming power of the 7.62 millimeter slugs. The chief petty officer caught sight of a determined enemy soldier who had been in a prone firing position located in the roots of a large tree. The man, in the process of taking a careful sighting on Gordon's midsection, died screaming when Popeye stitched him from neck to buttocks in two separate bursts.

Gordon looked at him. "Thanks."

"Right, Sergeant," Popeye replied grinning. "Let's do like Dinky Dow says—*kick ass!*"

The pair continued forward with the rest of the detachment until they halted. Then Falconi gave a silent "as skirmishers" signal by stretching out his arms. After the men had quickly, but quietly formed up, they moved back as silently as possible to the trail.

The Falcon's men found what they wanted when they got there.

The Pathet Lao killer teams—one from the front of the ambush site, and the other from the rear—had arrived at the scene of the main attack and now stood in the open trail looking around in chattering confusion.

They fully expected to see some bodies of the imperialist commandos lying in the path and to find others scattered around the jungle nearby. But they hadn't heard the explosions of the mines either.

The Black Eagles took careful aim on the milling group of enemy troops standing on the path. On the Falcon's command, their simultaneous fire raked the group, pitching the dozen Communist partisans to the earth in broken, bloody hunks of meat.

Archie Dobbs stepped out on the track. He noted a

moaning guerrilla among the cadavers. Archie laid the muzzle of his assault rifle at the base of the man's skull and pulled the trigger.

Then he walked over to Falconi with an apologetic expression on his face. "I led us right into this."

"Don't sweat it, Archie," Falconi said. He had checked the men. "We have no casualties."

Archie, disgusted with himself, shook his head. "I should've known something was wrong when there wasn't as much as an animal track on that path. The bastards must've swept it clean with branches to cover their footprints before they got into their ambush positions."

Falconi walked up to the despondent young sergeant and laid a hand on his shoulder. "Look at it like you dropped a pass during a crucial play, Archie. But it's the third down now. We've got another chance before we have to punt. You won't gain a damned thing by worrying about it. It's done. Just chalk it up as a lesson learned and go on from there."

"Right, Skipper. Thanks." He hesitated. "You still want me to take the point?"

"Hell, yes!"

Archie grinned. "Okay. Well, shit! Let's do like the ol' shepherd and get the flock outta here."

Archie threaded his way through the other Black Eagles who had stepped out from the trees to reform. He was relieved as hell that none of them had caught a slug. The worst hurts suffered were a few scratches added to the others they had gotten previously from charging through the brush.

"Hey! Hold up!" It was Calvin Culpepper. He had taken a quick look onto the other side of the trail. He trotted up to Falconi. "Say, Skipper. Them Pathet Lao strung out some Claymores in there."

"American mines, huh?" Falconi remarked. "I wonder where the little bastards got 'em."

"How's about takin' time for me and Popeye to get in there and pull a few out? They might come in handy."

"Good idea," the Falcon said. "I'll have Archie hold up. How long do you figure it'll take you?"

"Twenty minutes," Calvin said. "But I'd rather take a half hour. Safer that way."

"Go to it then."

The mines that Calvin and Popeye retrieved were officially known as M-18 A1s. They were designated as directional, fixed fragmentation types. They could be detonated either electrically or nonelectrically, and used as booby traps, regular land mines, or as controlled weapons. Rectangular with a slight curve, these dangerous little devices were deadly in a horizontal arc of 100 meters. There was one and a half pounds of C4 plastic explosive inside the plastic matrix to propel the 700 steel balls out into its killing range.

Calvin and Popeye also found the bandoleers the mines had come in. Within twenty-five minutes the two had rejoined the others with four Claymores stowed across their shoulders in addition to their other demolitions gear.

"We're ready to go, Skipper," Popeye said. "It's a damn good thing you had us charge into that ambush and surprise them little fuckers. If we'd gone in the opposite direction we'd be hunks o' hamburger right now."

"Right," Falconi said. He motioned to Horny Galchaser, the last man in Fire Team Alpha. "Pass the word up to Archie. We're ready to move out."

Once again the Black Eagles fell into the exhausting routine of slow travel through the jungle. Archie now led them off the trail, making their deadly journey tedious and numbing to the point that, after three hours, Falconi finally had to send word forward to halt their progress.

Archie hurried down the formation to the commander. "We stoppin' for a while, Skipper?"

"Yeah. The guys have had it, Archie." The Falcon looked closely at Archie's drawn face. "And so have you, ol' buddy."

"I'm a little tuckered," Archie admitted. "But I still got a lot of go."

Malpractice McCorckel took advantage of the break to pass out salt tablets and check all the canteens to make sure they were using the water purification pills he had issued them at the start of the mission. He also inspected feet for blisters, and noted the general physical condition of the detachment.

When he joined Archie and Falconi on the trail, he did not appear happy. "We got problems, Skipper."

"What's the matter, Malpractice?"

"A couple of the guys are starting to show symptoms of heat exhaustion," the medic said. "Chun Kim is the worst."

"Yeah, well, keep an eye on them," Falconi said. "If we have to, we'll carry heat casualties with us. At least we'll tote 'em as far as we can. I hope to God this situation doesn't deteriorate to the point where we have to eliminate any of our own guys."

"Me too, Skipper. But right now they need a good, long rest," Malpractice said. Then he shrugged. "I know we can't take the time. I'm just thinking out loud, that's all."

"We'll do our best for them, don't worry," Falconi said. He appreciated his medic's concern for the men. That's what made him so good at the job—and that's why they endured his mother-hen mannerisms with good-humored protests. Every member of the detachment also knew that Malpractice McCorckel genuinely cared about them.

Sparks Jackson set up his radio. "No sense in wastin' the opportunity, Skipper." He turned on the instrument and recalibrated the frequency before speaking into the microphone. "Black Eagle, this is Falcon. Over."

Falconi, Archie, and Malpractice intently watched the procedure.

"Black Eagle, this is Falcon. Over," Sparks repeated hopefully.

After several more attempts he shut the set down. Sparks shook his head slowly. "Couldn't raise 'em, Skipper."

"Prob'ly the Pathet Lao have closed in around ol' J.T. and Orville again," Archie said.

"Yeah?" Malpractice said. "Maybe they're squattin' in a POW cage right smack in the middle of some Red guerrilla camp."

Archie looked at Falconi. "What do you think, Skipper?"

Falconi sighed. "I'm thinking we've got to keep this rest stop as brief as possible. If we don't get back to those two soon, they most certainly are going to be either prisoners or swinging from a tree by their necks." He motioned to Archie. "In twenty minutes we'll have to get back to hauling our asses out of here."

Archie sat down and leaned against a tree. He was

immediately asleep. Like all good field soldiers he had developed the extraordinary talent of being able to nod off at a moment's notice. And twenty minutes of sack time would add another two or three hours to his energy level.

CHAPTER SEVENTEEN

The ringing phone echoed in hollow, persistent tones across the large expanse of the hangar.

Senior Master Sergeant Steve Padilla cussed under his breath and left the crew of mechanics he was supervising to amble over to the jangling instrument. He picked it up and spoke in a bored tone. "Maintenance Support, Sergeant Padilla spearing, sir."

"How are you, Steve?" came the voice on the other end. "This is Colonel Baldwin."

Padilla's face instantly broke into a wide grin. "Hey, Colonel! I'm doing fine. How's it going with you, sir?"

"Pretty good," Baldwin said. "Do you have any troop transports going through there right now?"

"Yes, sir," Padilla answered. He was the senior non-commissioned officer in charge of a high echelon repair and maintenance facility at Tan Son Nhut Air Base. "There's a coupla C-130s and a C-123. We've always got a couple here for repair or overhaul. What kinda aircraft capability are you looking for?"

"I need to tow a glider," Baldwin answered.

"Pardon me, sir?" Padilla said laughing. "But did I hear you right? You want to pull a glider around?"

"Sure do, Steve," Baldwin assured him.

"You got me confused, Colonel, but I'll take your

word for it, okay?" Padilla said. "You can explain it all to me later. And, don't worry, I got several planes that can do the job."

"Listen to me, Dan," Baldwin said urgently. "I need one of them. What are my chances of you putting off the return of some aircraft to its parent unit?"

"I could make a paperwork delay, Colonel." Then Padilla laughed. "You know damned well I can't say no to you. How soon do you need one?"

"Yesterday."

"Oh, shit! These babies won't be ready to fly for another day at least," Padilla said.

"Damn! What other kinds of aircraft do you have down there?" Baldwin asked.

"That's it, sir. Sorry. Just them three."

"Jesus, Steve. Couldn't you —"

"Hey! There's a C-47 over in the next hangar," Padilla said. "I forgot about it."

"What's the story?"

"Well, Colonel, it belongs to the South Vietnamese Air Force. I think the ol' bird was left here by the French," Padilla explained. "It's been deadlined and I ain't had a chance to look it over."

"Listen to me, Steve. This is damned important," Baldwin said. "Check that C-47 out *now*. See if it's flyable, or can be made that way. Then get back to me."

"Sounds like you really need that bird, sir."

"Lives depend on it, Dan. And that's no exaggeration."

"Okay, Colonel Baldwin, I'll hop to it." He hung up the phone and called over to his assistant, a squat, greasy-faced technical sergeant. "Hey, Moore, take over for a while. I'm gonna check out the goony bird next door."

Moore waved his acknowledgement, but added, "What the hell you think you're gonna do with that crate?"

"Get it in the air, baby!" Padilla yelled back walking out of the hangar.

"If there's any sonofabitch in this world that can do it, it's you," More said turning back to his own projects.

Steve Padilla had put in twenty-one years in the United States Air Force. A native of El Paso, Texas, he had been drafted in 1943 into the old Army Air Corps. A topnotch automobile mechanic, his initial aptitude testing at the induction center was so revealing of his natural talents, that even the army put him in the job he could perform best — aircraft mechanic.

As a youngster, Steve had loved fast cars. The sheriff of El Paso County was well acquainted with the boy's ability to take an old clunker, spend a few hours replacing parts and tuning the engine to perfection, and then turn it from a jalopy into a machine that could make a respectable appearance at any of the dirt track stock-car events in the state.

The only problem was that Steve Padilla didn't bother to enter his cars in bona fide races. He preferred to challenge other kids to drag his latest creations from intersection to intersection across town.

When rationing cut down the amount of gasoline he could purchase in the States, Steve would drive across the international border into Juarez to fill up his car with Mexican gasoline and to stock up on fuel in various containers for future use.

After numerous chases and run-ins, an armed truce of sorts developed between Padilla and the law. It was agreed that if he confined his racing activities to the dirt roads outside of town, the sheriff and his men would go ahead and let him drive like a maniac until he broke his fool neck in a high-speed crash.

The arrangement worked fine for both sides, though it was no secret that El Paso's various police agencies breathed long sighs of relief when they heard the youngster had been drafted and taken off to the army.

Steve Padilla's exposure to maximum-performance pursuit aircraft, such as the P-38 Lightning and P-51 Mustang fighters, brought him into a more sophisticated and serious area of motor mechanics than simply restoring some jalopy's functioning. These flying machines sported highly tuned engines which pulled them through the air at speeds that dazzled the mind of a young man of the 1940s.

He became a top notch aerial engine mechanic, never fully satisfied with the aircraft entrusted to him until it was tuned and pitched to absolute perfection. The fighter pilots, who were fortunate enough to have Steve Padilla as their crew chief, knew the airplanes they flew into combat were in the best condition possible.

One of these fortunates was a young hotshot flyer from Wichita, Kansas named Captain Winston Baldwin who became an ace, then a double ace, flying P-51s that were maintained under Steve Padilla's meticulous and loving care.

As Baldwin kicked the Mustang through the straining demands of dogfights against Hilter's dauntless *Luftwaffe*, the pilot knew that if there were any failure involved, it would be through his own errors or the superior flying and shooting skill of some German pilot — most certainly not from mechanical malfunctions.

161

Now Senior Master Sergeant Steve Padilla strolled into the hangar where the old C-47 sat neglected and lonely. He walked around the airplane noting the exterior. It seemed to be in good shape with no outward structural damage.

Next Padilla went inside and walked up the slanting fuselage to the cockpit. He worked the controls and they checked out to his satisfaction. Finally, the air force sergeant went back outside for one more quick exterior appraisal of the old goony bird.

He patted one of its wheel struts with genuine affection. "There, there," he cooed to it. "Stevie's here. No need to feel bad anymore."

Orville Hanover had to piss so bad he thought his back teeth would soon be floating.

He lay in the cramped confines under a bush, squirming uncomfortably while the nearby sounds of a Pathet Lao outfit filtered to his ears through the dense jungle growth. He tapped J.T. "Man, I gotta take a leak."

"Wait," J.T. whispered back.

"I can't!"

"You got no choice!"

Orville wiggled some more. "I don't think I can wait, J.T."

His older companion scowled at him. "Then piss in your pants for Chrissake!"

"No . . . I don't want to do that."

"You want one of those little fuckers to hear you?"

"No," Orville replied.

"Then either wait or go in your pants," J.T. insisted.

"I'm gonna sneak out and pee," Orville said. He wiggled from under the cover afforded by the brush.

"Orville!" J.T. whispered frantically. "Get your dumb ass back in here."

But Orville had already stood up and tiptoed several yards away into the dense growth of trees that surrounded their glider. He unbuttoned his trousers and almost groaned with relief as his bladder let loose its liquid burden. The growing release of pressure was almost sensuous it felt so pleasurable to him.

After he'd finished and rearranged his trousers, he stood there for several minutes. He and J.T. seemed to spend all their time either lying or squatting under or near that damned bush. Being able to stand up straight in an upright position caused his blood to flow in a different direction now, and he stretched by thrusting his arms over his head as far as they would go.

The comfortable feeling from the simple act was so good Orville was sure it was sinful.

Finally he lowered his hands to his side and took a careful look around before starting back to the hiding place. Orville walked carefully through the vegetation. He'd gone only about ten feet when he heard the unmistakable splatter of someone else urinating. He smirked at J.T.'s lack of control, especially after the guy had urged him to piss in his pants rather than take any chances. He headed directly toward the sound and stepped out into the small opening in the trees where the bodily relief was taking place.

The Pathet Lao, as startled as Orville, held on to his leaking penis and stared in transfixed fascination at the American.

Orville, acting under pure instinct, lunged forward and grasped the Red by his skinny throat and squeezed for all he was worth. Luckily for him, the guerilla had just finished nature's call so he didn't spray the determined attacker.

Orville could feel the Pathet Lao's Adam's apple slither under his thumbs as he continued to jam them into the guy's throat. The Red clawed desperately at the American's eyes, raking his cheek with his long, dirty fingernails. Orville rammed a knee into his opponent's testicles . . . once . . . twice . . . three times, still holding on to his neck.

The young partisan besides being smaller and skinnier than Orville was also badly nourished. His physical strength, no matter how desperate he became, could not match that of his slim, panic-stricken attacker. Orville closed his grip so tight that he now trembled with the effort.

Then he felt the windpipe collapse.

The Pathet Lao, his eyes rolled back and his tongue protruding, shuddered violently and then went completely limp. Orville, still holding on, fell to the ground with his burden.

It was a full five minutes before he finally released the fearful grip. His forearms felt as if they were burning now that his fingers had relaxed.

For several long moments Orville stared down at the kid he had just killed. Then he stood up and walked woodenly back to his companion.

"Jesus!" J.T. complained under his breath. "It's about time." He noticed Orville's strange expression and the fresh scratches on his face. "Hey, what's the matter with you?"

"I just killed a guy," Orville responded numbly.

"What the hell are you talking about?" J.T. demanded.

Orville recovered somewhat. "I was coming back here and I heard somebody taking a piss. I thought it was you and when I went over there it wasn't you."

"Of course it wasn't!" J.T. snapped.

"It was one of them Pathet Lao. I reached out and grabbed his neck and squeezed and squeezed until he fell down."

J.T. was silent for one long second. "What'd you do with him?"

"Do with him? Hell, J.T., the sonofabitch was dead," Orville said. "There wasn't anything else *to do* after that."

"Goddamn it!" J.T. cursed. "If those bastards find his body they'll know there's somebody else in this patch of jungle besides themselves."

"Oh, shit!"

"You didn't think o' that, did you?"

"No," Orville confessed. "I just wanted to get out of there."

"Well, we gotta go over there and drag him out of sight," J.T. said. He got to his feet. "C'mon and show me where he is, but stay quiet."

"Okay."

Moving more cautiously than usual, the two went back through the thick growth of rain forest vegetation to the place where Orville had encountered the Pathet Lao.

The little guerrilla still lay there. His eyes were wide open, looking vacant and unfocused in death, yet they seemed to Orville to cast an accusing glare at him. He turned away.

"Get his feet," J.T. said.

The two gingerly picked up the cadaver and moved it

deeper into the brush. They covered it with several layers of dead leaves and brush.

"There!" J.T. said. "Let's hope his buddies don't come prowling around too close looking for him."

Orville took note of the steamy weather. "He's gonna start stinking soon, isn't he?"

"Yeah," J.T. said. "And that means they'll eventually notice where he is even if they're not looking for him."

"Those guys had better get back here *fast!*" Orville said with a worried expression on his face. He looked at his companion trembling. "If they don't, these crazy bastards around here are gonna get us for sure. It's only a matter of time."

"Jesus Christ!" J.T. exclaimed. "Tell me something I don't know!"

The newly mounted blackboard was firmly fixed to the wall. Shiny and blank, it waited for the first mark of the chalk.

Lieutenant Colonel Gregori Krashchenko walked up to it and carefully wrote out a name at the top.

THE BLACK EAGLES

Line 01 — Captain Robert Mikhailovich Falconi
        Commanding officer
Line 02 —
Line 03 —
Line 04 —
Line 05 —
Line 06 —

He stepped back and smiled to himself. At last the information he'd been sent to dig out of the confused situation in Vietnam was beginning to be revealed to him. All he had to do now was to fill in the blank lines. His superiors in the KGB would reward him well if he was able to complete that portion of his assignment in record time.

The Russian's thoughts were interrupted by the entrance of his North Vietnamese counterpart, Major Truong Van. Truong held out the paper he grasped in his hand. "A message just arrived for us." He noticed the blackboard. "What is this about, Comrade Colonel Krashchenko?"

"That is the first name we have of that accursed bandit gang that has been plaguing our operations in this area. We have learned their unit designation and their commanding officer."

"Yes," Truong said enthusiastically. "Everything falls into place in military intelligence if you are patient and put the pieces of the puzzle together with determination and logic."

"Indeed," Krashchenko said in agreement. "It is almost like a chain. A random check for detached American officers in Southeast Asia led to a particular name. Since the man can legally be treated as a Soviet citizen, we had a further inquiry made about him and he turns out not only to be a member of the very unit we are trying to identify, but he is the commanding officer."

"And we shall learn more, Comrade Colonel Krashchenko," Truong said. "Our operatives in the south have guaranteed without reservation that we shall soon know all the gangsters assigned to the Black Eagles."

Krashchenko took the message that Truong had brought in. He read it quickly, his eyes lighting up. "Ha! An official combat report on a clandestine attack on the nuclear reactor site in Laos." He glanced at his North Vietnamese friend. "Who does that sound like?"

Truong pointed to the blackboard. "The Black Eagles, of course. What actions do we take, Comrade Colonel Krashchenko?"

"They have already done their damage. Evidently the bandits are still in the area. At this very moment, units of the Pathet Lao are in hot pursuit of them. It is imperative that we get our hands on Captain Falconi," Krashchenko said. "How soon can a special strike force be sent into the area?"

"That depends, Comrade," Truong answered. "Do you mean Pathet Lao or North Vietnamese?"

"A battalion of your regulars, of course," Krashchenko answered. "From the sounds of this report, it appears these Black Eagles are doing almost as they please over there."

"An infantry battalion can most certainly be dispatched immediately," Truong said. "It is only a matter of your making an official request to hasten the matter."

"Get me the necessary forms," Krashchenko said. "And I want to make sure that General Vang Ngoc is put in charge of the operation. The Black Eagles escaped his clutches on the Song Bo River. I'm certain he will be most diligent and dedicated to correcting that particular failure."

"Of course, Comrade Colonel," Truong said. "But I must respectfully point out that General Vang has too much rank to command a mere battalion."

"After the fiasco at Song Bo, he is lucky to have any rank at all!" Krashchenko snapped.

"You are correct," Truong said politely, "I will see to it immediately."

Krashchenko waited until Truong left the room; then he turned his attention back to the blackboard. If he not only identified the Black Eagles, but was in charge of the operation that destroyed them and brought in their leader as a prisoner, he could be assured of a generalcy when he returned to Moscow. He smiled at the name there.

"This is the beginning of your Swan Song, Captain Robert Mikhailovich Falconi!"

Chuck Fagin stepped into the outer office at almost the precise moment that Andrea Thuy hung up the telephone on her desk. The Eurasion woman looked up at her boss. "That was Colonel Baldwin at air ops."

"Have they got that C-47 fired up yet?"

"You know about that?" Andrea asked.

"Of course," Fagin answered. "I always have a listening antenna or two out. Now tell me, is Baldwin's plan a Go or a No-Go?"

"He hasn't the slightest idea until his mechanic calls," Andrea said.

"I tried to get a couple of Air America's grease monkeys sent over there, but it was like beating my head against a stone wall," Fagin said.

"Maybe if you called one of the air force units, they could spare somebody," Andrea suggested.

"Nope," Fagin said. "This thing that Baldwin and his old pal Padilla have come up with is strictly on the QT.

They're breaking a lot of the regs into little pieces. And, anyway, there is no way in hell the local fly boys are going to authorize pulling men from understrength maintenance crews to service a woebegone old C-47 in the hope it might be able to fly. Especially if they can't be told the reason why."

"I suppose there's a lot of work that has to be done on that airplane Baldwin wants," Andrea said.

"There sure is," Fagin told her. "Not to mention having to mount the retrieval hook under the fuselage so they can pick up the glider."

"Who's going to fly into the operational area?" Andrea asked.

"I don't know," Fagin said. "And I don't want to talk about it."

Suddenly Andrea's eyes lit up. "Baldwin is going to do it, isn't he? He said he would if he had to."

"I don't know a goddamned thing about it!" Fagin snapped.

"Everybody in SOG is aware that man is under direct orders to never, never fly again over enemy territory," Andrea said. "That's what caused him to get captured and sent to Garrison Three in the first place."

Fagin tried to change the subject. "Were there any messages for me while I was out."

Andrea ignored his question. "And you, you phony, are acting like you're completely in the dark about it."

"About what?" Fagin inquired with an innocent look on his face.

"By rights you should turn him in," Andrea said smiling. "But you won't do it, will you?"

"I asked if there were any messages for me?" Fagin repeated.

"Let me tell you something, Chuck Fagin," Andrea said with unabashed warmth, "the more I get to know you, the more I like working for you!"

C-47 air transports have been known by various names: Dakotas, Goony Birds, DC-3s, and Skytrains among others. They were the principal aerial workhorses during World War II and proved themselves to be reliable and efficient aircraft.

The C-47 could carry a 7500-pound load 1,500 miles at an airspeed of 185 miles per hour. At the extreme maximum, they could haul 27 paratroopers or 10,000 pounds of cargo through a flak-riddled sky.

When Senior Master Sergeant Steve Padilla went to work on the airplane in the South Vietnamese Air Force hangar, he found himself laboring on a pair of 1,200-horsepower Pratt and Whitney engines. These very same ones had been maintained through the ingenuity and devotion of a parts-starved French crew. They had cannibalized other C-47s to keep this particular bird flying on resupply missions during the Battle of Dien Bien Phu some ten years previously.

After that, the South Vietnamese took this well-proven airplane and increased its life of service through blind luck and the forgiving qualities of the C-47 itself. Although ignored for several months, the old bird had sat resolute in that hangar. It was almost as if the Dakota knew it would be wanted and needed again.

Thus, the veteran airplane seemed to have consciously fought against the encroaching deterioration brought on by the tropical climate that tried so hard to punish it.

Steve Padilla, weary and grease-stained, finally stepped down the the mechanic's stand after the final run of the engines. He had done the job mostly alone, but now and then during those long hours, one of his trusted off-duty mechanics, who couldn't resist helping put some life into the ancient aircraft, would sacrifice some of his beer-drinking and whoring time to lend a hand.

Sworn to secrecy, the air force men enjoyed the work and the challenge, but they were a bit confused by the large glider-retrieval hook that had to be mounted on the fuselage up toward the aircraft's nose.

Even Senior Master Sergeant Steve Padilla had no complete answer to the inquiries about the strange device.

Finally, at three o'clock in the morning, Padilla put a call through the military switchboard.

The voice that answered the call was sleepy, but there was a hint of tenseness in it. "Colonel Baldwin speaking."

"Sir, this is Padilla."

Now there was both apprehension and enthusiasm. "Yeah, Steve? What have you got for me?"

"Good news, sir. The bird is ready to fly."

"Hey! That's great!"

"What time are you going to want to make a test flight, sir? Padilla asked.

"We won't have time for one, Steve," Baldwin said.

"*We?*"

"Right, I figured you'd want to come along with me," the colonel added.

"I don't know, sir. I'm pretty well loaded down here right now," Padilla said. "Is this thing important?"

"It's not only important, Steve, it's unauthorized,

strictly against Air Force regulations and dangerous as hell!" Baldwin said.

Padilla laughed. "In that case, sir, you can count me in!"

Baldwin chuckled back into the phone. "Steve, I knew that was the criteria you would require. Hang loose. When this situation breaks open, it'll do so with a big bang!"

CHAPTER EIGHTEEN

Captain Falconi stood absolutely still behind the large tree.

He listened to the approaching footsteps, tightly holding on to the deadly stiletto in anticipation of its potential use. The Pathet Lao strode two paces past him, and Falconi stepped forward. He slid his left hand over the Red's mouth and nose, then he drove the slender blade of the dagger up into the man's kidneys.

The partisan struggled in the big American's grasp. His desperation made it impossible for Falconi to make a killing slash across the throat, so he drove the knife into the lower back once more. But the angle of the thrust was off and the slender blade broke on a rib.

The Red was dying, but doing it slowly. Falconi held on desperately as his victim struggled in his arms. The man finally managed to sink his teeth into the hand over his mouth. Now it was the Falcon's turn to feel agony. He held on as his blood mingled with that of the Pathet Lao. The next best course of action would have been to apply a forearm vise to break the man's neck, but the leader of the Black Eagles couldn't work himself into the proper position.

However, there was a sudden gush of blood over his hand, and the Communist guerrilla gave up the ghost.

The Falcon backed into the deep brush before lowering the body to the ground. He started to return to his original position by the tree, but the voices of several enemy soldiers warned him to stay hidden. A trio of guerrillas, chattering happily, strolled past him before disappearing into the jungle.

Falconi stepped from the leafy cover and made his way forward, walking slowly and with a great deal of care. He was in the middle of a large Pathet Lao unit that he estimated to be either battalion-sized or possibly made up of two companies. The rest of the Black Eagle Detachment waited a hundred meters away while their commander and the redoubtable Archie Dobbs each made single reconnaissances in an attempt to find a safe path through the Communist outfit that blocked their way back to the glider.

After ten minutes of slow moving, Falconi heard some more rustling in the brush. He changed his direction of travel slightly in order to stay in an area away from where the main concentration of enemy troops might be. Moving with the patience of a sloth, he finally found the source of the noise.

A two-man Pathet Lao observation post, manned by what seemed to be mere boys, had been established at the edge of a clearing. Falconi surmised that they faced away from their unit; thus a possible avenue of safe passage existed to their front. He pulled back fifteen meters and moved off to check out the surrounding jungle.

The captain found the passage he wanted, but it wasn't the best possible situation. Not far from the first post was a second. The latter one faced the former, giving indication that the Pathet Lao were set up in various perimeters of defense, each one able to cover the other.

He cursed under his breath. The whole damned operation seemed to be going from bad to shittier.

It took Falconi nearly three-quarters of an hour to get back to the Black Eagles. Malpractice McCorckel wasted no time in bending his ear as he entered the hidden position. "Skipper, these guys are deteriorating badly. And that goes for you and me too."

"It doesn't matter much," Falconi said. "All we need is the strength for one final effort. It'll be that or nothing. Is there anyone who might not make it?"

"I'm really worried about Chun Kim," the medic said. "He's a game little guy, but he was never given enough time to become acclimated to this area. They sent him here directly from Korea. He stayed at Tan Son Nhut only long enough to jump on the chopper and get flown to our base camp."

"Anybody else that bad off?" Falconi asked.

"No, thank God. But the rest of us are about ready to hit the skids," Malpractice said. "I wish there was a creek or something nearby. We could just sit in the damned water and lower our body temperatures for a while."

"We wouldn't have time anyway," Falconi said. He left Malpractice and walked over to Sparks Jackson. "Raise the glider."

"Aye, aye, Skipper," Sparks said. He cranked up the AN/PRC-41 and spoke hopefully into the microphone. "Black Eagle, this is Falcon. Over."

Silence.

"Black Eagle, this is Falcon. Over."

More dead air.

"Black Eagle, this is Falcon. Over." Sparks sighed. "Shit! I don't think I can get 'em, Skipper. They must be keepin' their heads down again."

"Keep trying, Sparks. The next couple of hours or so

176

depends on our being in contact with that goddamned glider," Falconi said. He looked around. "Is Archie back?"

"Not yet, Skipper."

"Send him to me the minute he shows up," Falconi said, settling down to take a quick nap. "We're just about to play our final hand in this game."

"I hope we got aces," Sparks said.

"At this point," Falconi said. "I'd settle for a pair of deuces." He drifted off into a fitful sleep with Sparks' voice droning in the background.

"Black Eagle, this is Falcon. Over."

The MP opened the door allowing Colonel Ngai Quang to step into the outer office.

Unsmiling, Andrea Thuy looked across her desk at the visitor. "May I help you, Colonel?"

"Yes, please," he said politely. "I must ask you to pardon this unannounced visit, but it is most important that I speak with Mister Fagin."

"Just a moment." Andrea got up and went into Chuck Fagin's office.

Ngai watched her appreciatively. He noticed the trim waist and shapely buttocks even under her army uniform. Her firm breasts were also apparent despite the martial attire. Ngai, at that moment, thought of how very much he would like to take her to bed. Eurasian women fascinated him as did blonde westerners. One of his fondest fantasies was to find himself in bed with a statuesque, yellow-haired white woman who was plump and much taller than he.

But the time Ngai spent on diversions was squandered on gambling rather than women — that was his real weakness: the mah-jongg table rather than the bed. And his sense of self-preservation added to this limitation of sin. He knew that any wild demonstration of weakness could lead to his assassination. Ngai, if he were ever deemed to have become completely unreliable, would be retired by a cyanide gas capsule. This method of causing a pseudo heart attack was a favorite of the KGB.

Andrea reappeared. "Mister Fagin will see you now, Colonel."

"Thank you," Ngai said, thinking how regrettable it seemed that Andrea Thuy wasn't blonde and heavier.

Chuck Fagin came around his desk and shook hands in a friendly fashion. "Nice to see you again, Colonel Ngai. Is there some way I might serve you?"

"Yes, Mister Fagin," Ngai said. "I am here without first informing you of my visit because of a phone call I received in my office. Higher echelon of ARVN has a special and most urgent request. They've ordered me to follow through on it with you personally."

Fagin was surprised. "Oh? And what might this all be about?"

"They require the names of the men serving with. . ."Ngai feigned straining his memory—". . . ah yes! Falconi . . . Captain Falconi."

"Who is requesting this information?"

"I am not at liberty to say, Mister Fagin," Colonel Ngai said. "Forgive me."

Fagin went back to his chair and settled into it with a thoughtful expression on his face. "May I ask what channel this request came through?"

"Of course," Ngai answered. "General Headquarters G-2."

He had actually received word of the need for this information the night previously at the mah-jongg parlor, and Tsing Chai had impressed him with the need for a rapid response. Thus, Ngai had been given no time to employ any ruses such as producing a phony message form to be put through regular channels. He was in a position where he would have to bluff Fagin into supplying him with the roster.

"We must confirm this," Fagin said.

"Again, pardon me," Ngai said smiling. "I am not permitted to reveal the source of this intelligence requirement."

"Then I most certainly will not supply the information," Fagin said.

A combination of anger and fear coursed through Ngai's emotions. Failure in obtaining the roster could very easily develop into a most nasty and dangerous situation for him. "I must remind you, Mister Fagin, this is *our* country in which you are operating."

"Which we're doing for *your* good," Fagin countered.

"I am sorry you do not trust our army," Ngai said coldly. "And I must inform you that your attitude will be brought to the attention of our highest command elements."

Fagin reached for his phone. "I am going to kick your request upstairs, Colonel Ngai. I cannot be responsible for dispensing such potentially damaging and dangerous information without proper authority and permission. Do you understand?"

"Of course, Mister Fagin!" Ngai said magnanimously. He breathed a silent sigh of relief.

The higher-ranking elements of the CIA and U.S. military intelligence would be far enough removed from the reality of the situation and would readily agree to supply the roster of the Black Eagles. They would do this for no better reason than to promote harmony and a spirit of cooperation between themselves and South Vietnamese authorities.

And, besides, Ngai was well known and trusted in the Americans' higher echelons. He smiled happily at Fagin. "Thank you so much!"

The trio of Black Eagles—Lieutenant Dinky Dow, Master Sergeant Gordon, and Sergeant Dobbs—sat in a semicircle around their commander.

Falconi's voice was low and urgent, emphasizing the state of his emotions. He traced a path across the map laid out on the ground. "That's it, guys—Freedom Avenue. A straight line from our position here to that fucking glider. And it'll take us directly between two Pathet Lao outfits. We've got that one route and no other way to make it back."

He was interrupted by Sparks Jackson who sat with his radio a few yards away. "I still can't raise J.T. or Orville, Skipper."

"*Shit!*" the Falcon cursed. "Okay, Sparks, bypass them and contact the aircraft. Tell SOG air ops to have their guys over that LZ in exactly two hours."

"Aye, aye, Skipper. But what if we ain't there when they show up?"

"I don't even want to think about it, Sparks." Falconi turned back to the others. "We'll be going under the guns of several Pathet Lao outfits. If we're lucky and quiet enough we'll be able to sneak through, If not, we'll be running a gauntlet of fire. And I mean that literally. It could mean bad casualties. Whoever's left over will set up the retrieval rig for the aircraft to snag the glider. If there aren't enough guys, they'll have to forget it and E and E back to friendly territory in any manner they can."

Falconi was interrupted again, this time by Malpractice McCorckel. "Falcon, Chun Kim has just about had it. He's passed out. Shallow breathing, hardly any pulse, and his skin is hot and dry."

"What are his chances?" Master Sergeant Gordon asked. The Korean marine was in his fire team.

"If he doesn't get proper treatment soon, he'll die," Malpractice said with a worried expression. "He's got two or three hours, that's all."

"Just like the rest of us," Falconi said sardonically. "It doesn't make much difference. Rig up a litter and you and another man carry him as far as you're able."

"How about getting Horny to help me? Or will it mess up his fire team?" Malpractice asked.

"We'll be fogetting team integrity from this point on," Falconi said. "Use who you want."

"Skipper!" Sparks Jackson called over. "The aircraft is laid on with an ETA on the LZ of 1630 hours."

"Right," Falconi said checking his watch. "Okay, I've already briefed Calvin and Popeye on what they're supposed to do. Archie will go with them ahead of the rest of the detachment with a half-hour lead. They should be set up on the LZ by the time we arrive there. Let's get the word to the rest of the guys and have 'em ready to go on time. We'll let Malpractice and Horny rig up a litter for Chun Kim before we move out."

"I'll alert Calvin and Popeye," Archie Dobbs said, slipping a fresh magazine into his AK-47. "I wonder if any of these operations will ever go smoothly."

Falconi winked at him. "Hell, Archie! Nobody ever

181

said this job was going to be easy."

General Vang Ngoc watched as the soldiers of the 327th Infantry Battalion loaded onto the East German Garant-30K trucks.

The unit had originally been slated for duty in South Vietnam, but severe casualties suffered in clashes with the clandestine imperialist bandit gang in their rear area had caused their commitment to be delayed. They had been returned to their barracks in Hanoi which they now prepared once again to leave.

But this time they were bound on a special mission to Laos.

The general turned to his adjutant and smiled almost sarcastically. "Isn't it amazing, Comrade Captain, how one lone Russian KGB lieutenant colonel can get more done in North Vietnam than a mere indigenous general?"

The other officer stuck a cigarette between his lips and lit it before replying. "And all in the name of honorable vengeance, Comrade General."

"I suppose it is only proper that the one unit that took such a mauling from . . . from . . ." He thought for several moments. "What is the name of the enemy outfit?"

"The Black Eagles, Comrade General," the adjutant replied promptly. The one reason he had been chosen for the job was because of his thoroughness and excellent memory for detail.

"Yes! The Black Eagles," Vang said. "A dashing name for a gang of freebooters, hey?" He laughed nervously. "But, as I was about to say before, it is only correct that the 327th Infantry be allowed to administer the death blows to them."

"They lost many men," the adjutant reminded his commander.

"And so did I on the Song Bo River," Vang said. "I suppose that is why the Russian chose me for this operation. He felt I would be properly motivated. Even if my rank is much too high to command a single battalion."

"Undoubtedly." The adjutant felt very ill at ease. General Vang, having been taken from his brigade and put in command of a unit one-fourth its size, was obviously in a state of disgrace. Being too closely identified with him could turn out to be disastrous for any young officer's career.

"And only the KGB could arrange for the necessary aircraft to transport my new unit into Laos," Vang continued. "What sort of flying machines have been placed at our disposal, Comrade Captain?"

"Russian Li-2 transports, Comrade General."

"How very generous of our comrades to the north," Vang said. "Well, shall we join the brave soldiers of the 327th? We mustn't hold up this grand operation."

"Of course, Comrade General. We should be landing at the Xiangkhoang air base within two hours."

As they walked to the street where the small Soviet UAZ-69A command car awaited them, General Vang spoke once again. "I must admit, Comrade Captain, that despite the humiliation of this assignment, the KGB colonel was absolutely correct in one of his assumptions."

"What is that, Comrade General?"

"I want, with all my heart and being, to crush those devils in the Black Eagle detachment!"

"Phaong! Phaong!"

J.T. and Orville instinctively drew themselves farther into the bushes as the singsong voices of the Pathet Lao drew closer.

"Phaong!"

Orville edged closer to J.T. and whispered in his ear. "What the hell do they mean with that word?"

"I think I just figured it out," J.T. said. "It's probably the name of that guy you killed awhile ago. They must be his buddies looking for him."

"Oh, shit!"

"Yeah!"

There was a rustling in the brush that drew closer to them. The sound of the guerrillas angry conversation also became louder as they poked around looking for some sign of their missing comrade.

"Phaong!"

Orville felt cold stabs of fear. The last few days of lying in the middle of battalions of barbarians had been bad enough, but the approach of the moment of final confrontation was almost unbearable.

Rustling movements sounded in the grove of trees that had offered them cover and separation from the enemy camps. Now, as if in a bad dream, the first Pathet Lao stepped from the tall stand of jungle vegetation and stopped in stunned surprise.

Standing in front of him in all its glory was an aircraft. It was painted in a camouflage pattern that was strange. Yet at the same time it jogged something in his memory. The soldier called out to his comrades. The two joined him, and their eyes also opened wide at the unexpected sight of the glider.

"An airplane!" one exclaimed.

"Does it belong to one of our battalions, comrades?"

another asked.

The first soldier continued staring at the unusual sight as he mused aloud. "It is strange this painting on it . . . yet I have seen it before, but where?"

Suddenly one of the others exclaimed. "It is like the uniform the Yankee we hung was wearing. It is the same colors and stripes!"

"It is his airplane then," another surmised. "That is how he arrived here."

"Maybe there are others around," the first soldiers said. "We must search."

They held their Kalashnikov assault rifles at the ready as they poked the vegetation around the glider. They were persistent as they prodded the bushes with their feet and with the muzzles of their weapons.

The first soldier worked his way to the center of the area and, reaching carefully inside a palm frond, pushed it aside. He yelped in surprise at the sight of the two Americans hiding there. He knew but a few words of English, but they were adequate for J.T. Beamer and Orville Hanover to understand him.

"Come out! Come out!"

Slowly, fearfully, they raised their hands and stepped from their concealment into the open.

CHAPTER NINETEEN

Always maintain a good rapport with the enlisted personnel.

That had been Lieutenant Colonel Winston R. Baldwin's basic philosophy in his many years of service in the United States Air Force.

And it had always paid off handsomely — especially lately.

As the colonel worked the controls of the C-47, Senior Master Sergeant Steve Padilla sat in the copilot's seat on the other side of the cockpit from him. The twin engines of the aircraft fairly purred as their propellers bit air and pulled the machine through the Asian sky.

Getting the Dakota in shape to fly had been the biggest favor an enlisted man had done Baldwin lately. The second best token of good will he had received from a noncom was the phone call to the C-47's hangar where he and Padilla had been waiting fretfully.

A communications sergeant deftly informed him that the Black Eagles had requested the pickup that same afternoon at 1630 hours. Rather than cancel the rescue operation as he had been ordered, the radioman not only confirmed it, but passed the word on to Colonel Baldwin to execute the mission as originally planned.

They were now one hour from the ETA — the Estimated Time of Arrival.

Falconi raised up enough to catch sight of the Pathet Lao machine-gun nest. The muzzle of the Russian Vz-59 Czechoslovakian automatic weapon was situated to cover a wide arc in front of the position. When he was sure it was safe, he signaled to Duncan Gordon.

Gordon, moving swiftly but silently, stole through the bushes in front of the enemy soldiers and disappeared into the jungle on the other side.

A few minutes later Falconi again waved his hand. This time Tom Newcomb passed through the danger zone.

The hairiest moments had been when Malpractice McCorckel and Horny Galchaser, with the unconscious Chun Kim slung between them on a poncho attached to a long pole, stole past the Pathet Lao machine gunners. Every Black Eagle had been tensed for the worst, but the two had pulled it off with flying colors.

Finally, when Lightfingers O'Quinn had made it, Falconi had his turn. He would be the last. If he made it okay, they could proceed to the LZ for the rendezvous with the pickup aircraft.

Then there would be a new set of troubles to deal with.

Falconi tensed himself as he waited for the right moment. Then he made his move.

J.T. Beamer and Orville Hanover stood with their hands raised. The three Pathet Lao who had captured them moved closer. The one who was the apparent leader barked some orders they didn't understand. This was followed by the Americans being grabbed and roughly pushed face-first to the ground. Then the two prisoners' arms and hands were bound tightly and painfully behind them.

The Reds used the short lengths of rope they always carried. In accordance with their army's regulations, before going into combat they tied these bonds around their ankles. This facilitated having their cadavers dragged away in the event they became casualties.

"Shit!" Orville hissed.

The senior guerrilla snarled and kicked him hard in the ribs. Then the two were pulled to their feet. Again, the Pathet Lao used his limited English. "Go! Go! he exclaimed in his high-pitched voice. He pointed in the direction he desired, and before the prisoners could respond, they were kicked and pummeled into movement.

Baldwin pressed the left rudder and eased the wheel into the same direction maintaining a slight backward pressure to keep the C-47 from slipping into a downward attitude during the turning maneuver. "How far out are we, Steve?" he asked.

Steve Padilla checked the map and watch. "I'd say about a half hour, sir."

"Ever see a glider retrieval?" the colonel asked.

"Nope," Padilla answered. "You ever made one before?"

"Can't say that I have," Baldwin remarked. "But it ought to be interesting as hell, huh?"

"Yeah!" Padilla said with a short humorless chuckle. "For everybody concerned!"

"Sounds like a lack of trust in my flying abilities, Sergeant," Baldwin said in mock severity.

"Sir, I have great confidence in your flying ability, the internal combustion engine and *la Virgen de Guadalupe* — but not necessarily in that order."

"Do you think this What's-Her-Name Virgin is watching over this operation?" Baldwin asked.

"*La Virgen de Guadalupe* takes care of all us Mexicans, Colonel," Padilla answered.

"What about a *gringo* pilot?"

"Just be glad you're with me," Padilla replied.

Orville Hanover's hands were already growing numb despite less than five minutes in the cruel bonds that held them tightly immobile. He strode, with his head mournfully cast down, in the direction indicated by the Pathet Lao. His mind was already filled with pictures of the torments that awaited him as a prisoner of the semi-civilized Communist barbarians who were now his Lords and Masters. He heard a slight scuffling behind him, and he could picture J.T. Beamer falling and being kicked back to his feet.

"Orville," J.T. called out.

The young soldier kept walking. There was nothing he could do to help his friend.

"*Orville!*" J.T. was more insistent.

Orville stopped and waited to see what would happen. He hunched his shoulders for the blows he was sure would quickly follow.

"Goddamn it, Orville! Turn around!"

He did as he was told, then stood in gape-mouthed wonder at the sight before him.

Archie Dobbs, Calvin Culpepper, and Popeye Jenkins were untying J.T. At their feet lay the three Pathet Lao. The Reds, silently knifed and taken out of action, were soaked in their own blood.

"C'mon over here, Orville," Calvin said, his ebony face split in a wide grin. "I'll get you outta them ropes."

"Holy Toledo!" Orville exclaimed. "What're you guys doing here?"

"We're the advance party," Calvin explailned. He slit the bonds with his knife. "Looks like we got here just in time too."

Orville rubbed his wrists to get the circulation flowing through them once again. "Where's Captain Falconi and the others."

"On their way," Archie Dobbs said. "We got a lot o' work to do before ever'body gets here. We got a retrieval rig to put up, and these demo experts of ours are gonna plant some Claymores around here. And then we gotta move that glider into position."

"Yeah," Popeye said. "Not to mention keepin' about ten thousand fuckin' Pathet Lao off our asses in the meantime."

"I couldn't raise 'em, sir." Steve Padilla put the microphone back in its place on the instrument panel. "Are you sure they're going to be there?"

"They radioed for a pickup, so that's the assumption I'm going to make," Colonel Baldwin said. "The only problem is that the tactical situation gives us one — and one only — chance to dive across that LZ and snag the glider. If they're not in position when we make our run, they're dead ducks."

"Maybe they already are, sir."

"Yeah."

"And maybe it'll be us who ends up as *patos muertos*," Padilla added.

"What does that mean?"

"It's Spanish for Dead Ducks," Padilla said.

"No kidding?" Baldwin repiled. "Now how far out are

190

we?"

"Fifteen minutes, sir."

"Right. At 1630 I'll make the run," Baldwin said.

Padilla nodded and looked out the window. The old warning cry of many a kid's game swept through his mind:

Ready or not, here we come!

Falconi stared across the open expanse of the landing zone. He could easily discern where the glider had been hidden away. The blind of brush thrown up there had died now, leaving a stark, yellow-and-brown square in the tree line.

He stepped back into the jungle where the others waited for him. "It looks okay so far. We'll skirt the LZ around the edge to the aircraft. I hope like hell that those guys over there are ready." He looked at Malpractice and Horny. They squatted on the ground with Chun Kim lying between them. The Falcon was concerned. "You two look tuckered out. I'll get you some relief."

"I'll stick with it, Skipper," Malpractice said.

"Me too," Horny echoed.

"Okay, suit yourselves." Falconi motioned to Dinky Dow. "Lead the way. We'll follow."

Gunfire broke out across the open space.

"Oh, hell!" Falcon exclaimed. "The guys over there must've gotten spotted."

"Hot damn!" Dinky Dow yelled. "Kick ass!"

The little Vietnamese took off running across the LZ toward the area where the glider was hidden. The others immediately followed as Malpractice and Horny struggled with their burden.

"We're five minutes out, Colonel," Steve Padilla announced.

"Roger. I'll make the turn for the run in," Baldwin said.

"Sir. . ." Padilla spoke with some hesitation in his voice. "Don't you think hitting that LZ at *exactly* 1630 is cutting it awful close?"

"Might be just the opposite," Baldwin said. "They may be sitting down there at this very moment sweating our ETA."

Padilla was silent for several moments. "Hell, sir," he said finally. "You and me both been in the service over twenty years. Did you ever know of anything to be ready or to come off *early*?"

Baldwin glanced over at him, then turned back to flying the airplane. "Am I about to get some advice from a senior noncommissioned officer?"

"Yes, sir," Padilla said. "Cut 'em some slack."

Baldwin sighed. "Okay. Change that ETA to 1640."

Archie Dobbs turned from firing at the Pathet Lao and looked at the remainder of the Black Eagles Detachment as they crashed into the jungle where he, Calvin, Popeye, J.T. and Orville had formed an impromptu defensive position.

Falconi joined him. "What's going on, Archie?"

"Fuckin' Reds stumbled into Calvin and Popeye settin' up them Claymores," Archie said. "We had to return fire. We didn't get a chance to set up the glider."

"We'll do it now," Falconi said. He motioned to J.T. and Orville. "Get that rig out of the glider and position it." He grabbed the two nearest men to him — Tom Newcomb and Lightfingers O'Quinn. "Give 'em a hand."

"Right, Skipper!" Lightfingers said.

The four rushed off to the task while the others poured fire at the attacking unit of Pathet Lao.

"Damn!" Falconi said checking his watch. "1629."

Gordon Duncan raked the brush ahead of him with the AK-47. Two Reds who had charged forward were stopped in their tracks by the bullets. They toppled into the bushes like bloody bundles of rags. "Sir, you think they can get that rig up in sixty seconds?"

Falconi didn't bother to answer. He spotted a partisan trying to climb deftly and rapidly into the concealment offered by the palms of a tall tree. He took careful aim and cut loose with a short burst of fire. The guerrilla's arms flew out from the slamming impact of the bullets into his body and he fell backward into a clumsy dive on his way to the ground.

Out on the Landing Zone, the quartet worked rapidly. First the various lengths of the collapsible retrieval poles were quickly fastened together. Then the long loop of nylon rope was threaded through the snap fasteners located on the very ends.

Tom Newcomb and Lightfingers each took one of the devices and stuck them deep in the soft earth of the meadow they had landed on. The only weight the apparatus had to bear was that of the rope; thus the two Black Eagles had only to force the sharpened ends deep enough into the muddy dirt to stand erect.

When it finally stood there ready, the affair resembled a pair of rather sloppily erected football goal posts.

In the meantime J.T. and Orville had torn down the camouflage blind to clear the way for pulling the glider out into position. By the time this was done, Tom and Lightfingers joined them. All four slid the light aircraft across the slippery expanse of grass. It moved easily on its waxed skids and within a short time it was positioned in front of the poles. J.T. grabbed the loose length of nylon rope between them and quickly fastened it into the glider's tow hook.

It was 1632 hours.

Falconi, directing the fight against the enemy unit closing in on them, ordered the detachment to close up. He yelled at Malpractice, "You and Horny get Chun Kim into the glider. On the double!"

"Roger, Skipper!" Malpractice answered. The two Black Eagles, their adrenaline pumping like sixty and overcoming all adverse affects of the near heat exhaustion they suffered from, jogged clumsily from the trees out to the aircraft with the Korean between them.

1635 hours.

Gordon moved close to the detachment commander. "They've evidently given us some breathing room on the tow plane's arrival time, sir. We'd better set up a rear guard while the others get aboard that glider."

"Right, Sergeant. The guys that stay here to cover the withdrawal might not make it out of here," Falcon said.

"Yes, sir," Gordon said. "I volunteer."

"Me too!" It was Archie Dobbs nearby.

"I'll make the third of our intrepid trio," Falconi said. Then he yelled at the others. "Fall back to the glider—
now!"

It was 1638 hours.

The retrieving aircraft could be heard at that moment, its engines cranked up as it swooped in to grab its waiting load.

Orville and J.T. were in the pilots' positions and the other eleven Black Eagles had buckled themselves into the passenger seats.

1639 hours.

Falconi, Archie, and Gordon broke off the attack and raced for the glider. Archie Dobbs hit a hidden depression in the ground and went down. Falconi, who hadn't seen him, continued running madly, but Gordon stopped and turned back.

"Get outta here, Sergeant!" Archie yelled.

"Shut up and get off your ass," Gordon countered. The big master sergeant grabbed Archie by the collar and hauled him up so hard the scout's feet left the ground.

Still clinging to Archie, Gordon scrambled to the door and flung him in. The he dove for the entrance.

The C-47's retrieval hook, wide open and gaping, hit the nylon rope strung between the poles. It snapped shut as the Dakota streaked on, instantaneously taking up the slack and jerking the glider into the air.

Master Sergeant Gordon Duncan, half in the glider but with his legs dangling on the outside, grabbed hold of the nearest seat brace as the flimsy nonpowered aircraft slashed through the air behind the tow plane.

The Pathet Lao, screaming in rage and confused frustration, rushed out from the jungle and cut loose at the escaping aircarft with their AK-47s.

CHAPTER TWENTY

Cold air sped past Master Sergeant Gordon's legs as he dangled outside the glider.

He had grabbed hold of the seat brace nearest to the door as the flimsy, motorless craft slashed through the sky behind the tow plane.

Archie Dobbs and Calvin Culpepper eased themselves down the steeply slanted deck of the glider toward the team sergeant. At the same time there were zapping sounds as bullets from the ground slapped into the aircraft.

Gordon's wrists were finally grasped hard by Dobbs, while Calvin helped by lying across the scout's legs to weight him down. Horny Galchaser added his own contribution to the effort by sitting on the floor and holding onto Calvin's ankles. They all strained against the centrifugal force of the climbing aircraft as they fought to keep Gordon from slipping away and falling to the jungle far below.

But Orville Hanover was having his own troubles.

An enemy round had snapped one of the control cables to the rudder. This device was used to steer the glider in tow. Without it, the motorless flying machine had slipped into the buffeting storm of prop wash behind the C-47.

"I can't hold it!" Orville screamed to J.T. sitting next

to him.

J.T. pressed the microphone button and spoke rapidly into the instrument. "Mother Bird, this is Black Eagle. Over."

Senior Master Sergeant Steve Padilla's voice responded to the call. "Go ahead," he said without ceremony.

"We got no rudder," J.T. said. "We're bouncing around back here like a puppet on a string—a broken string. Over."

"Roger, wait," Padilla said. After a few moments he came back. "The pilot says we'll slow as much as possible, but we gotta keep up speed or stall. And that'd be the end of both aircraft. Okay? Over."

"I guess it's gotta be okay," J.T. said.

There was a noticeable drop in the rpms of the C-47 as it leveled off. That gave Calvin Culpepper the opportunity to get to his knees and pull back hard on Archie's ankles. Horny dropped down and wrapped his arms around Calvin's waist to help out.

The black demolitions sergeant looked over his shoulder at Horny. He grinned. "I love you."

"I love you too," Horny shot back. "Now shut up and pull."

Inch by agonizing inch they eased Gordon forward until the master sergeant was finally able to slip one foot inside the fuselage. He used this as a lever and pushed hard, helping the others until he was finally through the door.

Gordon stood up and walked past Archie, Calvin, and Horny. He patted each on the head. "Thanks." He reached the empty seat beside Falconi and sat down. The team sergeant looked at the Black Eagles' commanding officer for a moment; then he grinned and spoke aloud, "Nobody said this job was going to be easy!"

Falconi, his body bouncing from the turbulent ride, nodded his complete agreement. "Sergeant Gordon, you took the words right out of my mouth!"

Colonel Robert Donaldson, United States Air Force, stood disbelievingly in front of Chuck Fagin's desk. He would normally handle any business within SOG's military bureaucracy by office telephone, but the situation that had been brought to his attention was unusual enough that the senior officer of air operations wanted to check things out personally.

Especially if there was a good chance he would have to be covering his ass in the event of an official investigation.

Donaldson chose his words carefully as he spoke. "Now let's just put everything in order before we get into this subject too deeply. It would be too easy to confuse matters and cause future misunderstandings if we don't."

"Right," Fagin agreed.

"Okay. Now the primary thing we've got going here is a mission involving the Black Eagle Detachment of SOG," Donaldson said.

"You're correct," Fagin said. He was rather amused by the discomfiture he sensed in the officer. Donaldson stood ramrod straight, his hawkish nose and close-cropped gray hair giving a distinct impression of a no-nonsense attitude.

"And this detachment is commanded by Captain Falconi?"

"Indeed," Fagin answered. "Captain Robert Mikhailovich Falconi. I don't know his serial num—"

"*Service* number," Donaldson corrected him. "Items of equipment have serial numbers, personnel have service numbers."

"I stand corrected," Fagin acknowledged. "As I was saying . . . I don't know his *service* number by heart, but I'm sure it's here somewhere in the files if you need it."

Donaldson missed even this pointed and obvious sarcasm. "That's perfectly all right, Mister Fagin. I can get it later for the record."

"Major Thuy outside can give it to you," Fagin went on. "Also a physical description and probably a fingerprint card on Captain Falconi."

Donaldson began to sense a lack of cooperation developing. "Let's get back to this case. The Black Eagle Detachment was sent on a mission which they had accomplished except for the exfiltration. And that phase of their operation, according to the message logs in air ops, was canceled."

"I am aware of that," Fagin said.

"Yet at this moment that aforementioned attempt of getting them out of the operational area is underway," Donaldson said.

"That is what we've been able to determine from monitoring communications," Fagin told him. "I requested confirmation from your office as per SOP."

"But I authorized no such flight," Donaldson said. "And there's not one scrap of paper that indicated that I have. I am as surprised as anyone that the Black Eagles are being brought back—how do you CIA fellows say?—out of the cold?"

"I generally call it bringing them home."

199

"Mmmm, I see," Donaldson said. "Fine . . . then it would be proper to say there is a South Vietnamese Air Force C-47 bringing Captain Falconi and his men home."

"Yes, I am quite happy to be able to confirm that," Fagin remarked. He pulled a cigar from his desk and lit up. "And it would appear that it is being piloted by an officer from your command."

"My goddamned executive officer!" Donaldson snapped suddenly getting angry. "I'm tired of beating around the bush, Fagin. What do you know about all this shit?"

"Nothing."

"Liar!"

Fagin remained nonplused. He took a couple of slow drags from the stogie. "I will go on record as stating that I am in complete ignorance on whatever activity *your* office is engaged in at the moment concerning the Black Eagles."

"Goddamn it, Fagin! I want you —"

"And there's no sense in discussing it with me," Fagin insisted. "I might add, that the thing won't be called off now."

"I don't want to call it off either," Donaldson said. "But I do want to find out who's responsible."

"The only reason you want to know is to save your ass," Fagin stated coldly. "My God! You should want to put your executive officer in for a decoration."

Donaldson started to speak again, but Major Andrea Thuy opened the door from the outer office. "There's a phone call for you, Colonel," she said.

"Thank you."

Fagin shoved his telephone across the desk. "You can

take it on this one if you like."

Donaldson picked up the instrument. "Colonel Donaldson speaking. . .right, I know about it . . . Yeah . . . yeah . . . okay . . . Keep me posted, Sergeant." He hung up and looked at Fagin. "That was my commo chief. He says that radio reports from the C-47 indicates the Black Eagles are in deep shit. Their glider is bouncing behind the tow plane like a busted kite."

"Any further information on the glider's condition?" Fagin asked. "Can it take much buffeting?"

"Jesus Christ, Fagin! What the hell do you think?" Donaldson asked. "The goddamned thing is a frail, hastily built orange crate that's been exposed to long periods of tropical air. I'd give it the life expectancy of the proverbial snowball in hell."

Steve Padilla leaned out into the prop blast and looked past the tail of the C-47. At first the sky appeared to be empty, but suddenly the glider whipped up into view, shuddering at the end of the tow rope. Then, just as quickly it was whisked away out of sight.

He watched the frightful gyrations of the fragile aircraft for several more minutes before pulling his head back into the relative quiet of the fuselage. Padilla walked back to the cockpit and slid into the copilot's seat.

"How does it look?" Baldwin asked.

"Pretty damned bad, Colonel," Padilla said seriously. "Those poor bastards are getting beat to death back there."

"Well, I can't back off on the throttle," Baldwin reminded him. "It's taking every ounce of horsepower we've got just to fly. And if this old crate starts coughing and stalls out, we'll pull them down with us."

Padilla's eyes quickly scanned the instrument panel. "That's not the only thing wrong around here."

Baldwin, fighting the controls, groaned. "What else do we have to worry about?"

"Starboard engine's oil temperature is climbing," Padilla said. He glanced out the window at the offending motor. "I was worried about that. And towing that god-damned glider isn't helping much."

"How long can we last?" Baldwin asked.

"I don't know, sir," Padilla answered. "This baby needed a complete overhaul. I did the best I could under the circumstances and in the time I had. But it wasn't good enough maybe."

"Nobody could have done better," Baldwin said sincerely. "I've been around you long enough to know that."

"We may have to get that glider off our asses," Padilla said.

"No way," Baldwin responded.

"Sir, if we haul 'em until we conk out, then we'll both go down. They'd crash anyway," Padilla said. "At least we could save our asses and this bird, too, if the glider cuts loose."

"You really want to do that, Steve?" Baldwin asked pointedly. "Just let those guys loose over this jungle? Look down there. There's not one goddamned place for them to land within their glide range."

"Hell, Colonel, I'm a mechanic giving advice," Padilla said. "I didn't say I wanted to follow it."

Baldwin glanced over and winked at him. "I didn't think so."

Padilla grinned back; then he rechecked the oil temperature. He figured he would soon know if it were true or not that *la Virgen de Guadalupe* watched over the welfare of Mexicans.

The WAF secretary glanced up from her desk at the same moment that Colonel Donaldson returned to the air ops office. He motioned to her to follow him into his office. The young woman, knowing both her commander and her job well, grabbed a dictating pad and pencils before reporting to him.

The colonel, obviously agitated, had just sat down when she joined him. "I have a couple of important letters that must go out, Sergeant," he said testily. "And they must be carefully worded."

"Yes, sir," she replied. Donaldson had depended on her skills as a diplomatic writer on several previous occasions. "What problems are we dealing with today?"

"The first one will be to SOG headquarters. I wish to disavow any prior knowledge of a completely illegal and unauthorized flying mission undertaken by Lieutenant Colonel Winston R. Baldwin."

"Fine, Colonel," the WAF said cheerfully. "And what is the second?"

"A letter of apology to the Republic of South Vietnam for the wanton destruction of one of their aircraft."

The starboard engine of the C-47 began to emit smoke. Padilla turned from the window and glanced fixedly at Baldwin. "Decision time, sir."

The colonel nodded. "Right. Fly her for a while and let me talk to the glider."

Padilla, while not an expert pilot, had taken whatever opportunities he could in the past to fly various types of aircraft. He took the controls and kept the Goony Bird on a straight, level flight.

Baldwin spoke into the microphone. "Black Eagle, this is Mother Hen. Over."

J.T. Beamer's voice came back. "This is Black Eagle. Over."

"How's the ride back there? Over."

"It's getting rougher, Mother Hen. We lost our rudder, as you know. But there's been other structural damage. We can't be sure but we think the ailerons are jammed. We won't know 'til we get out of your prop wash and can fly properly. Over."

Baldwin cursed silently to himself. But he kept his voice calm. "I understand, Black Eagle. We have problems too. There's a good chance we may lose our starboard engine. If it goes, this baby won't have the power to haul you. We'll have to cut you loose. Understand? Over."

"Roger, Mother Hen." J.T. made no attempt to conceal his nervousness. "How soon will that shit come off? Over."

"Can't tell," Baldwin said. "I'm going up for altitude. That way when it happens you'll have a better run to a landing area. It'll help us too. With any luck at all, we'll come out of this smelling like roses. Over."

"Roger, Mother Hen. Any idea how far we are from our base camp? Over."

"We haven't had time to run any navigational checks due to the problem with the engine. But I'm maintaining a straight course in that direction. Out."

"Roger. Let us know when to get off tow. Out."

Baldwin took the controls back from Steve Padilla. He eased forward on the throttle and pulled the wheel back to begin a gradual climb.

"That's gonna cut the life of that engine, Colonel," Padilla said.

"Yeah," Baldwin said grimly. "I suppose it will."

"Would you care for some *nuoc che*, my dear Dai Ta Ngai?" Tsing Chai asked politely.

"*Khong. Cam on ong*," Colonel Ngai Quang said politely refusing the offer of tea. He had been summoned to Tsing Chai's house. This was not only unusual, but he had barely been given time to dress by the burly messenger who had delivered the curt invitation. "Is there something I can do for you?"

"Of course," Tsing Chai said. "And I can see you are impatient to find out what it might be."

"Forgive my directness," Ngai said with a slight bow. "But I fear a repeat of tonight's activities may call me to the security police's attention."

"A reasonable worry on your part, Dai Ta Ngai," Tsing Chai said with a smile. "And, thus, you must be aware of the importance of having you visit me."

"Yes. Of course."

"You have been asked to monitor the Black Eagles, and to keep us informed of their activities," Tsing Chai said. "Now we ask that you increase your responsibilities where that group is concerned."

Ngai acknowledged his acceptance of further orders with a slight bowing of his head.

"You are to foment a plan in which these bandits can be killed," Tsing Chai said. "And when—"

"Forgive my interrupting you," Ngai said with a smile. "But such action may very well not be necessary."

"You have news?"

"Yes. I was going to let you know tomorrow during

our regular meeting. The Black Eagles have begun the withdrawal phase of their latest operation, but are not expected to survive the effort. This is timely information that I received by telephone from my senior staff officer not an hour before your messenger arrived to escort me here."

"You are certain of this, Dai Ta?"

"The report is from SOG headquarters," Ngai emphasized. "And their chance of survival has been rated nil at best."

"Ah! I will pass this intelligence through our net," Tsing Chai said. "And you may consider the mission of their destruction on stand-by. If, by some miracle, they survive the unsurvivable, we will reinstate the planning for their permanent removal from this vexed and troubled world."

J.T.'s airsickness increased slowly but steadily as the glider bounced through the air behind the C-47. Several of the Black Eagles had already given in to their queasiness, and the deck of their flying coffin was slick with vomit.

The radio crackled and Steve Padilla's voice filled the hissing void. "Black Eagle, this is Mother Hen. Over."

"Roger, Mother Hen. Go ahead," J.T. said.

"You'll go off tow in five minutes," Padilla instructed him. "As soon as you're loose we'll feather the ailing engine and make a try for home. Your own landing area at the base camp is on a magnetic heading of one-thirty-seven. Over."

"Roger. I just hope that's the direction we can turn this fucking glider," J.T. said bitterly. "Out."

They continued their erratic flight until once again

the radio came to life. This time it was Baldwin. "Okay. There's no more putting this off. Good luck, you guys. Prepare to go off tow. Over."

"We're ready," J.T. said. "Over."

"On zero. Five, four, three, two, one—*zero!*"

"Off tow!" J.T. exclaimed. At the same time he pulled the release knob.

The glider slowed and steadied down into a reasonably steady flight. Orville Hanover tried a right turn. The controls were sloppy and the aircraft failed to respond. He gingerly turned the wheel to the left. The glider barely heeled over.

"All we got is a left turn," he announced to J.T.

J.T. glanced through the windscreen. "And the base camp is off to the right. You'll have to make an almost complete three-sixty. Go for it, Orville. While we still got some sky under us."

"Right!" He fought the controls over, and their craft barely responded.

"Try some rudder," J.T. suggested.

"What fucking rudder?" Orville asked disgusted. The glider wheeled slowly through the sky, dropping rapidly. "We gotta get some weight outta this thing."

"Right," J.T. yelled. He left his seat and hollered at the airsick Black Eagles. "Start tossing shit outta here. Weapons, equipment, boots . . . everything!"

A quick relay line was set up and the men passed down their weapons. Archie Dobbs, by the door, grabbed the items as they were handed to him and threw them into the void outside the fuselage.

Orville, his eyes wide with fear, tipped the nose down to get the wind passing faster over the wings. The maneuver worked well—too well. He had misjudged the distance to the base camp's landing strip.

"Give me spoilers!" he yelped. "Goddamn it, J.T., more spoilers!"

He yanked the wheel back and mushed out a bit; then he let the nose sink again.

"This is it!" J.T. hollered back. "Ever'body sit down and buckle in!"

They hit hard and bounced once . . . twice . . . then flipped over on their backs as the Black Eagles slammed against each other and the bulkheads.

A Special Forces security guard, who had watched the bizarre landing, cautiously approached the overturned aircraft. He jumped back when the first man emerged. It was Archie Dobbs wearing only his GI shorts. He had thrown everything else out in the frenzy to lighten the glider.

The guard recognized him. "Hi ya, Archie. How's it going?"

"Oh, pretty good, I guess," Archie answered. Then he quickly added. "What time's chow?"

CHAPTER TWENTY-ONE

A hot breeze swept indolently through the window and into the office. Lieutenant Colonel Gregori Krashchenko, gazing outside into the humid afternoon, mopped at the sweat on his brow with a soiled handkerchief and then replaced it in his rear pocket.

Behind him, seated at his desk, Major Truong Van finished his careful reading of the report. He lay the thick document down and glanced up at his companion. "This doesn't make any sense at all, Comrade."

Krashchenko turned and leaned against the sill. "I was hoping you could understand what they were trying to say."

"What sort of aircraft would it be that leaps up at another which passes closely overhead?" Truong asked. "I have never heard of such a thing."

"As far as I know, no such flying machines exist. But the Pathet Lao commander was very explicit and clear in what he saw," Krashchenko remarked. "Whatever he is talking about was the manner used by the Black Eagles to escape. We must figure it out."

Truong turned his gaze to the blackboard. The Black Eagles roster was now filled out. Twenty-four hours previously the names of every member of the detachment had been sent to them through their operatives in South Vietnam. These had also been forwarded to KGB headquarters in Moscow for further processing.

Truong's thoughts were interrupted by the phone ringing. He answered it, and listened to the speaker on the other end of the line for a few moments before he spoke. "I see. Wait a moment, please." He motioned to the Russian. "Comrade Colonel Krashchenko, it is the Operations Bureau at headquarters. They are calling to let us know that General Vang and the 327th Infantry Battalion have returned to Hanoi. They would like to know if the unit is to be released to its regular duties."

"Of course not!" Krashchenko snapped. "They are to be put on stand-by status until further notice. There is no telling how, where or when those bastards the Black Eagles will strike next. The 327th will be used against them the moment they show up again."

"Yes, Comrade Colonel." Truong relayed the message, then hung up. "Is that the only action we are going to take against them? To simply wait?"

"Of course not!" Krashchenko snarled as pictures of his vanished general's shoulderboards flashed in his mind. "I fully intend to direct a program against them in the south as well. I have already requested additional funding and personnel from Moscow."

Truong smiled to himself. He was secretly amused by Krashchenko's anger and discomfort. But he also knew that the man's determined efforts, backed up by the deadly espionage and assassination skills of the KGB, would soon bring the activities of the Black Eagles and the lives of that detachment's members to a destructive end.

As if to emphasize Truong's thoughts, Krashchenko spoke aloud while studying the roster. "A vigorous and determined program of complete elimination will be launched in the immediate future."

Lieutenant Colonel Winston Baldwin knocked on the door of his boss at SOG's air ops office. He stepped inside. "You wanted to see me, Bob?"

"I sure as hell do," Colonel Robert Donaldson said angrily. "Sit down!"

Baldwin did so, smiling easily. "You seem upset about something."

Donaldson's face was a grim mask. "I could have you court-martialed, Winston. Dishonorably discharged from the goddamned service, imprisoned, fined, and . . . and . . ."

"How about shot?" Baldwin asked unconcerned. "Or flogged, flayed, and fried, along with the loss of my lending privileges at the base library?"

"You disobeyed orders, Winston," Donaldson said. "You flew over unfriendly territory in a plane that didn't even belong to us — and you didn't even have proper authorization or permission to use it."

"Before you get too deep into this chewing out, I'd like to find out something," Baldwin said. "How are the Black Eagles? The last I saw of them was when we flew over that camp of their's and they cut the glider loose to land. Then Padilla and I returned to Tan Son Nhut."

"They're okay," Donaldson said. "Suffering from heat exhaustion, but evidently all healthy. But all that is beside the point. You risked your neck after the United States government went to all kinds of trouble and expense to get you sprung from that North Vietnamese prison camp."

Now it was Baldwin's turn to lose his temper. "I don't give a good goddamn how much *trouble and expense* the fucking government went to," he said angrily. "The reason I'm out of the hands of the Commies was because of the efforts and sacrifices of a magnificent bunch of guys. And if you think for one minute I regret helping them after they'd been abandoned, you're out of your mind!"

Donaldson clenched his teeth so hard his jaw ached. "I can see there's no sense in speaking further to you about it."

"There sure as hell isn't!"

"You're being sent back to the States and retired, Winston," Donaldson said. "And that's being done under my personal recommendation. I won't have a man on my staff in a sensitive operation like this who can't control his emotions."

"*Yes, sir!*" Baldwin, knowing he could do absolutely nothing about it, stood up and saluted.

Donaldson calmed down. "If it's any consolation to you, there'll be a promotion to full colonel before the paperwork goes into effect."

"Fuck the promotion," Baldwin said. "I'm concerned about Sergeant Padilla."

"Relax. Absolutely nothing will be done to him." Donaldson returned the salute. "You're dismissed."

Baldwin went back to his desk to gather up his personal effects. He really wasn't too surprised and, deep in his heart, didn't blame Donaldson a bit.

Even if it did mean he had gotten forced out of the air force he loved so much, Lieutenant Colonel Winston R. Baldwin would have done it all over again.

He slammed his few possessions into an attache case, then looked angrily at the others in the room. He started to say something, but decided it would be of no use.

Lieutenant Colonel Winston Baldwin went to the hat

rack and grabbed the air force blue service cap. He looked at the American eagle insignia mounted on it. Then he smiled to himself.

"Yeah! You damned betcha I did the right thing!"

There was a rapping on her door and Major Andrea Thuy pressed the newly installed electronic opener on the floor next to her chair to admit the caller. When the visitor entered, she leaped up and rushed around the desk to fling her arms around him.

Captain Robert Falconi returned the embrace and kissed her firmly and passionately on the lips. Finally, they broke apart and he smiled at her. "I'm sure glad to see you."

"Oh, Falcon! I didn't think I would ever be with you again!" The well-trained operative fought her emotions and only allowed a slight quivering of her lips to betray the feelings of joy and relief that surged through her. "Will you be free tonight?"

"I should be turned loose as soon as I finish with Fagin," Falconi said.

"In that case, don't waste time." Andrea took his hand and led him to the CIA case officer's door. She knocked and then opened it, literally shoving the large man through into the inner office.

Fagin's eyebrows went up at this unusual entrance. "Are you really that anxious to see me, Falcon?"

Falconi grinned. "Sure."

"Well, I can save you some time on this visit," Fagin said. "The full poop on your mission came through. And the Russians, while mad as hell, aren't squawking aloud about having that nuke plant site destroyed. They sure as hell don't want any publicity about the venture. It would be very embarrassing for them. And it looks like they won't be renewing their efforts in that line either."

"Good," Falconi said. "That's what we wanted."

"J.T. Beamer is reported back in Texas," Fagin said. "With the money the Agency gave him for this operation, he plans on getting back into the glider business in a big way."

"Sailplane business," Falconi corrected him. "He builds sailplanes, not gliders."

"Whatever," Fagin said with a shrug.

"And what about our young friend Orville Hanover?" Falconi asked.

"We pulled some strings and he's back at Fort Dix, New Jersey, waiting to be processsed out of the army on an early discharge," Fagin said.

"Great," Falconi remarked. "Now that we have the good stuff out of the way, let's turn to the least pleasant subject I want to discuss with you."

"I know, I know," Fagin said wearily. "You want the reason why your guys are stuck out in that B-Team camp instead of allowed some R & R, right?"

"Right! Those guys haven't had any time off since Operation Song Bo," Falconi said.

"I have to take the full blame for that, Falcon. There's a situation that's developed I don't like," Fagin said. "I've been forced to turn over a full and complete roster of the Black Eagle Detachment to South Vietnamese intelligence. There's something about the deal that ain't kosher, and until I clear up a few matters I don't want any of your men—or you—wandering about as potential targets."

"Jesus Christ, Fagin!" Falconi exploded. "Don't bullshit me about your warm concern for us. You're more worried about any compromise regarding our operations here in SOG, aren't you?"

"You are so fucking right," Fagin said coldly. "Now I want a full, written report from you on Operation Laos Nightmare. Then you can hop on that chopper waiting for you at Tan Son Nhut Air Base and get the hell back to your detachment."

"While I have your attention, Fagin," Falconi snapped. "How about filling me in on Colonel Baldwin."

Fagin sighed. "Damn, Falconi, it seems like just about everything I have to tell you today is going to piss you off!"

"Let me have it," Falconi said.

"Baldwin is being retired," Fagin said. "I don't like it any better than you do. I think it's a bum rap too. But at least they're promoting him to full-bird colonel before he's turned out."

"Maybe I should be glad to get back to that B Camp with the boys," Falconi said. "The air seems cleaner out there somehow."

The Fort Dix, New Jersey MP detachment responded to the emergency call by dispatching a jeep and two of their biggest men to the scene of the disturbance.

When they arrived at the Separation Center, the military policemen were told that a soldier had gone beserk inside, causing the building to be evacuated. They could hear him screaming in rage and smashing things. Now and then objects came flying out through the windows.

"What the hell's going on in there?" the senior MP asked.

A veteran sergeant, the post reenlistment NCO, answered him. "I was giving this kid who was due a discharge, the standard reenlistment talk like everybody goes through. It was just the typical pitch to try and make him choose the army for a career. But he suddenly went crazy. He started hollering and throwing stuff around. He went completely bananas!"

"Okay, okay," the MP said trying to appear as professional and polished as possible. "Let's get the facts. What's the guy's name?"

The sergeant checked the papers he had fled outside with. "He's a specialist fourth grade named Orville Hanover."

"And what'd you say to him that set him off?" the MP asked.

"I was just using some psychology and appealing to his manhood when he said he didn't care to reenlist," the sergeant explained. "I only asked if he'd decided not to stay in the army because he was afraid of going to Vietnam."

CHAPTER TWENTY-TWO

There was a mood of absolute gloom in the Black Eagles' bunker. The night before they'd gotten drunk.

But not with the usual good humored beer guzzling of men who are celebrating the end of a dangerous job.

The drinking they had done was as angry and volatile as the boilermakers they consumed. Each and every Black Eagle was pissed off, disappointed, and sporting bad attitudes that were steadily growing worse.

It had all started when they were informed they would be allowed no R&R—Rest and Recreation—after their return from Laos.

They had taken their liquor quietly, their drunkenness sullen and restrained. Then, one by one, they had either passed out or simply staggered to their bunks and gone to sleep.

Now they lay or lounged around their stark living quarters with terrible hangovers. The men's heads throbbed and their stomachs were queasy, but their ire was still as strong and persistent as on the night before.

The thunder whistle shrilled outside once . . . twice . . . and several more times in impatient blasts.

"What the fuck?" Archie Dobbs demanded.

"It's Sergeant Gordon," Horny Galchaser said.

"Goddamn him and that . . ." Archie let the words trickle off to nothing. "Oh, what the hell, guys? He proved he's got balls and don't mink riskin' his ass for us. Let's go outside and see what he wants."

The ten men staggered up out of their sandbagged domicile to form up in front of their detachment sergeant. When they stepped into the sunlight, each and every one blinked his eyes at the strange sight that greeted him.

Master Sergeant Duncan Gordon stood there wearing his boonie hat and his jungle boots—and nothing else.

"Hey, Sergeant Gordon, you're buck naked!" Calvin Culpepper exclaimed.

"Uniform of the day," the master sergeant said with a grin. He held his thunder whistle in his hand. "I want you guys to come with me."

Confised and befuddled, they followed him around the bunker to the back of the structure. Gordon pointed at the ground. "Look there."

A hole, six feet wide, six feet long, and six feet deep with its sides straight and true, sat in full view of the detachment.

"Jesus!" Archie Dobbs said. "Who dug that Six-By?"

"I did," Gordon answered. "For this specific purpose." He took the thunder whistle and tossed it into the depths of the hole. "Gone forever, boys." Then he went to the entrenching tool stuck in the ground beside his creation and began filling the excavation in.

The Black Eagles watched him for several moments; then the meaning of what he was doing finally sunk in. Horny Galchaser laughed loudly. "Hey, Top! I'll go get my entrenching tool and give you a hand, huh?"

"Me too, Top!" Malpractice McCorckel added.

"Yeah!" Calvin Culpepper also said. "Wait for me,

Top."

The entire group rushed back to the bunker and returned to give Gordon a hand. Within moments, dirt flew as the thunder whistle was covered under the growing pile of soil.

"I gotta confess something, you guys," Gordon said as he swung his small shovel. "I dug this right where Archie had already done his. It was easier that way."

Archie Dobbs stopped working and burst out in a wild cackle. "Hell, that only proves one thing—you're only human, Top!"

More laughter followed as the Black Eagles continued their task of sending the thunder whistle to its last resting place.

They would soon be drunk again, but this time not because of anger over having no R&R.

This would be their official welcoming party for the new top kick—Master Sergeant Duncan Gordon . . .

. . . a Black Eagle at last.

EPILOGUE

The Old Man squatted on his haunches in the village square and stared mournfully down at the dust.

He had known war for over twenty years now. First the Japanese had come to form what they termed their Sphere of Co-Prosperity with the peoples of Asia. The Old Man and his fellow villagers had endured the Nipponese Empire's brand of administration and government until the end of World War II. Then the Sons of Heaven had been driven back to their home islands to resume their lives under the benevolent occupation and tutelage of their conquerors. As soon as they had been picked up and dusted off by the Americans, they began to enrich themselves manufacturing automobiles and electronic gadgetry based on transistor technology.

But the situation wasn't so pleasant in Indochina. The immediate postwar period was marked by the emergence of a new brand of tormentor who appeared in the guise of national liberators. This fresh batch of troublemakers called themselves the Viet Minh and proclaimed to people like the Old Man and the inhabitants of the little hamlet that they had come to deliver them from the clutches of the French oppressors. These strange nationalists, who practiced and peached a political philosophy as foreign as that of France, brought the war into the very huts of the village. They forced the people to hide arms, food, and other supplies for them. At the same time they took many young men away from them for indoctrination and training so that they would have the privilege of fighting and dying in this new war of independence.

Naturally, when the French soldiers came around in their campaign against the Viet Minh, they would sometimes find the things hidden under the huts of the villagers. This would mean quick and severe punishment despite the most vocal and sincere protestations of innocence or good intent. In a space of only three years, this small farming community had been burnt down no less than seven times.

Yet the only thing these unfortunate people asked of all the combatants was to leave them alone and allow them to grow enough rice to survive. "Why not take the struggle into the city where there are many more people?" they begged.

"Because *you* are the true revolution!" the Viet Minh had answered.

And the French had to fight there, because that was the place where the Communist guerrillas preferred to make the war, thus the Old Man and his people found themselves stuffed down a meat grinder—and it was their blood and their flesh coming out the other end.

Now the Old Man glanced up at these new soldiers who had recently arrived in the settlement. They spoke a language he did not understand, and these strangers made their wants and demands known with inarticulate grunts and shouts which were emphasized with kicks and punches.

The young women had already been raped. They had

221

been herded into one of the larger huts and the soldiers enjoyed them for a couple of hours before tiring of the sport. These women, shamefaced and disgraced, had rearranged their clothing as best they could for modesty's sake. This was difficult because the soldiers, impatient in their lust, had ripped the apparel from their bodies. The ravished women, bruised and in some instances beaten, lowered their eyes and returned to their homes. Each had endured at least three of the foreign soldiery.

The Old Man had a deep secret. He could not only read and write in his own language, but in French as well. He had found it to his advantage to conceal this from all the warring factions involved in this enigmatic struggle, and none of the villagers had betrayed him. His knowledge of the colonial power's language now helped him to recognize who these new soldiers were. Each sported cloth strips sewn over the breast pockets of his uniform. One of these was obviously the man's name, but the other, proudly mounted on the left side of the jackets, was black with gold letters that spelled out: U.S. Army.

The Old Man knew they were Americans and that, in this year of 1964, their presence was growing in Viet Nam.

The senior officer wore cloth insignia sewn to his collar. Now that the enjoyment of the women was over, he barked a few terse orders and his soldiers herded all the younger males into a group at the far end of the cluster of huts. The Old Man, looking ancient and frail, had been left with the women and children.

The village men were driven with rifle butts into a tight group as other soldiers, their weapons ready, formed up in a semicircle around them. More orders were barked and the invaders aimed their rifles at the packed mass of rice farmers. Some, realizing what was going to happen, held out their hands in imploring gestures for mercy.

But suddenly there was rapid and loud staccato rifle fire.

The slugs slammed into the hapless prisoners, the force of the impacts throwing them into each other as the steel-jacketed rounds tore into their bodies and they fell to the ground like bloody rags.

A couple of the men, who had been missed or only slightly wounded, made a break for the safety of the nearby jungle. They only got a few meters before a fresh fusillade slammed into their backs, spinning them around to fall face up between two outlying huts.

It seemed strangely quiet after the firing had stopped.

One of the soldiers, wearing chevrons on his arm, looked from the carnage to the officer. He snapped to attention and saluted. *"Ist das alles, Herr Hauptmann?"*

The officer nodded. *"Ja. Nun Ich Mochte Feldlager gehen."*

Two hundred kilometers to the southeast of the village where the atrocities had been committed, the Black Eagles sweltered and stagnated in their sandbagged bunker.

At that particular time, as they tried to numb the monotony with warm beer and stale jokes, the detachment had absolutely no knowledge of the massacre of the villagers or how it would affect their lives. But even as they did their best to bear up under the monotony of being stuck in a Special Forces B-Team camp far out in the boondocks, the gods of war in Valhalla, were laboring at

223

their looms, busily weaving future patterns of violence.
Operation *Asian Blitzkrieg* was in the works.